Resurrection Men

T. K. WELSH

· DUTTON CHILDREN'S BOOKS ·

DUTTON CHILDREN'S BOOKS

A division of Penguin Young Readers Group

Published by the Penguin Group

Penguin Group (USA) Inc., 375 Hudson Street, New York, New York 10014, U.S.A. / Penguin Group
(Canada), 90 Eglinton Avenue East, Suite 700, Toronto, Ontario, Canada M4P 2Y3 (a division of Pearson
Penguin Canada Inc.) / Penguin Books Ltd, 80 Strand, London WC2R 0RL, England / Penguin Ireland,
25 St Stephen's Green, Dublin 2, Ireland (a division of Penguin Books Ltd) / Penguin Group (Australia),
250 Camberwell Road, Camberwell, Victoria 3124, Australia (a division of Pearson Australia Group Pty
Ltd / Penguin Books India Pvt Ltd, 11 Community Centre, Panchsheel Park, New Delhi - 110 017, India /
Penguin Group (NZ), Cnr Airborne and Rosedale Roads, Albany, Auckland 1310, New Zealand (a division
of Pearson New Zealand Ltd) / Penguin Books (South Africa) (Pty) Ltd, 24 Sturdee Avenue, Rosebank,
Johannesburg 2196, South Africa / Penguin Books Ltd, Registered Offices: 80 Strand, London
WC2R 0RL, England

CIP Data is available.

Published in the United States by Dutton Children's Books,
a division of Penguin Young Readers Group
345 Hudson Street, New York, New York 10014
www.penguin.com/youngreaders

Designed by Jason Henry
Printed in USA / First Edition
1 3 5 7 9 10 8 6 4 2
ISBN 978-0-525-47699-3

For Olivia

ACKNOWLEDGMENTS

I would like to thank Maureen Sullivan for her ongoing faith in me; Richard Abate for his insistence that I stretch my wings; my friend, Dr. Matthew Snow, for his medical insights and suggestions; Vanessa and Carl, Alexander and Benjamin for their unstinting support; and, most of all, Olivia, whose love has helped to resurrect my heart.

RESURRECTION MEN

The body-snatchers, they have come
And made a snatch of me.
It's very hard them kind of men
Won't let a body be.

You thought that I was buried deep
Quite decent like and chary;
But from her grave in Mary-bone
They've come and bon'd your Mary!

The arm that us'd to take your arm
It took do Dr. Vyse,
And both my legs are gone to walk
The Hospital at Guy's.

I vowed that you should have my hand,
But Fate gave no denial;
You'll find it there at Dr. Bell's
In spirits and a phial.

As for my feet—my little feet
You used to call so pretty—
There's one, I know, in Bedford Row,
The other's in the City.

I can't tell where my head is gone,
But Dr. Carpue can;
As for my trunk, it's all packed up
To go by Pickford van.

The cock it crows—I must be gone;
My William, we must part;
But I'll be yours in death, altho'
Sir Astley has my heart.

Don't go to weep upon my grave
And think that there I'll be;
They haven't left an atom there
Of my anatomie.

Mary's Ghost
HOOD'S WHIMS AND ODDITIES
· 1826 ·

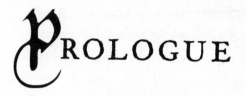

PROLOGUE

SEPTEMBER, 1852

VIRGINIA WATERS

SURREY, ENGLAND

IT RAINED. It had been raining for a week, and the roads were choked with mud, black mats of fallen autumn leaves, with flinty stone and blebs of sod, soaked clots of black dismembered branches. The carriage charged along the slippery lane, careened and coursed, pulled by three geldings and a mare, dark as the night through which they ran. It was almost nine o'clock, and they were very, very late.

Wrapped in a tattered jet-black cloak, the ancient coachman scanned the sky. Bruised thunderheads rolled soundlessly aloft, heavy as breakers on the strand. He turned and stared into the darkened landau. Inside, his master, the corpulent Marquess of Stanton, was diddling his latest conquest. A young brunette with doelike eyes and skin as white as fog, her head reclined against the velvet seat, her throat exposed, her mouth half open and her raspberry-colored lips aquiver. The coachman leered. He watched as the marquess pawed the girl. He strained to get a better look when, suddenly, the horses whinnied nervously. A bright white fork of lightning split the sky. A thunderclap barked back. The muddy lane revealed itself and, without warning, without a moment's chance to turn or pull back on the reins, a boy appeared before him.

The coachman cursed. He yanked the tracers, tried to break. A Stygian darkness choked the lane. There was a muffled thud, a bump, a scream. The coachman felt the landau grind across the object in its path. There was another bump; then, nothingness. The horses slowed, declining to a trot.

"What the blazes!" the marquess cried within.

The coachman reached out for a headlight as the horses finally stopped.

"You there," the marquess said. The coachman had been a member of his lordship's staff for almost seven months, but the marquess had yet to learn his name. "Coachman, what say you?"

The coachman turned and looked into the landau. "I fear we've struck someone, your lordship."

The marquess rolled his eyes.

The coachman slipped the headlight off its post and lifted it aloft. He could see nothing through the rain. He jumped down from the landau and looked about the undercarriage. Nothing. The horses pawed the ground. Shielding his eyes, the coachman checked their legs with care, one after the other. They appeared to be unscathed.

"Hurry up, man," the marquess said. "We're late."

The coachman sloshed around the carriage. In the dim glow of the headlight, he could just make out a solitary boot. It was worn and small—the footwear of a child. He stooped and was about to pick it up when something caught his eye. A rust-red rivulet ran lazily along the lane. Blood! He straightened up. He stared into the night. Just then, another bolt of lightning creased the sky. There! Two dozen yards away the frame of a young boy was curled up in a heap. The coachman groaned. He dashed across the lane, bent down upon one knee, and reached out with a wizened hand. The boy moaned softly as the coachman touched his neck. "He lives, your lordship. He lives!" Without waiting for an answer, the ancient coachman stripped the cloak from his broad shoulders and wrapped it around the broken frame. "There, there," he said. "You'll be all right, lad." Then he lifted the boy and dashed back to the landau.

The Marquess of Stanton was staring out the window. He had a flat round face, a pair of tiny light gray eyes, set close together, and a short flat nose. "What do you think you're doing, man?" he said.

The coachman was trying to open the side door. "He's 'urt terrible, your lordship. We should lie him down inside, sir."

"In here? Has the rain rinsed your wits, man? He'll bleed all over the upholstery. Just leave him. Someone else will be along, I'll warrant, soon enough."

"Poor dear." The lady with the raspberry-colored lips leaned forward, gazing down upon the shattered body in the coachman's arms. "He's just a boy," she said. "We can't just leave him, Percy."

The marquess looked indignant. "Pray tell, why not, Melissa? Look at what passes for his clothes. He's obviously a vagabond."

"But he'll die," she answered.

"One urchin more or less," the marquess answered with a pout.

"Please, your lordship. Have pity, sir," the coachman said.

"Don't be so heartless, Percy. I'll think of nothing else tonight if we just leave him here." The lady reached out for the door.

The Marquess of Stanton snatched her by the wrist. "If the price of your attention is a moment's dalliance . . . You are a little shrew, aren't you, Melissa?"

"But a soft and scented one," she said, pulling her hand away. "And one who would well please you."

The marquess laughed. He turned back toward the coachman. "It is your fault I find myself so used," he said. "Well, hoist him up onto your seat, then, if you must. I will not soil my clothes for one the likes of him."

The young girl leaned against her suitor's chest. "Oh, Percy. You are a decent fellow, after all," she said.

"So I've been told," the marquess answered as the landau shuddered into flight. "On more than one occasion."

Dr. Lambro sat at his kitchen table, listening to the rain. He was supping on a pair of apples and a chunk of cheddar, washed down by a flagon of warm stout. The rain pounded the thatched roof. A copper pot sat in one corner catching a steady drizzle of rainwater that dripped in from above. He eyed it suspiciously and sighed.

His was a simple cottage: a small sitting room in front, sparsely furnished; a mid-sized kitchen with a blazing hearth and roasting spit, plus the table at which he sat, ringed by four chairs; and above, on the second landing, two more rooms—the master bedroom, and the other for his two children, Mary and Nicholas. All in all, it was not a very grand house. Although well loved and respected by members of the hamlet, Dr. Lambro was a man of simple tastes. He never charged more for his services than his neighbors could afford. Indeed, he was as likely to be paid in eggs and pigs and chickens as in coin. But he wouldn't have it any other way. Such was his ilk.

He took a last bite of his apple and thought about the old English saying: *Ate an apfel avore gwain to bed, makes the doctor beg his bread.* He smiled a bittersweet smile. The adage was truer than most knew, he mused. Orchards were plentiful in the district. Perhaps that was why the bag of coins he'd secreted under a flagstone in his cellar was so light.

Dr. Lambro stood and stretched. It was almost nine o'clock and he was tired. But his wife was visiting a sick child down the lane, and he was loath to go to bed before her. Even after all these years, he felt an unbridled need to protect her. Not that she needed his protection; she was both spirited and strong. And yet . . . old habits died hard. He had loved her with all his heart from the first moment he had seen her.

A tall and gangly man, Dr. Lambro had the thick dark hair, strong jaw, and piercing hazel eyes of his forebearers. He was dressed in a simple cotton shirt, malachite green, with a bloodred kerchief round his neck and dark twill trousers. His hair was cut short, and although he had just turned thirty-four, it was already graying at the temples. His life had not been easy, and it showed.

Just then he heard a pounding on the kitchen door. Dr. Lambro turned. *Who could it be at this hour? Certainly not his wife,* he thought. The door was always left unlocked. "Come in," he said.

The door burst open. Colonel Maxwell, his neighbor, stepped through the doorframe, carrying something in his arms. He was soaked from head to toe. Behind him Dr. Lambro spied another man, quite fat, with a flat round face, wearing a woolen coat, a dark blue cutaway, and a silk top hat. The stranger was hovering under an umbrella carried by an old man with a lantern. Beside him stood a lady in a turquoise cape and bonnet.

"Thank God you're home," said Colonel Maxwell. "There's been an accident."

Dr. Lambro stepped up. He looked down at the bundle in Colonel Maxwell's arms. It was a boy, no more than nine or ten. A small line of blood slipped from his lips as his head lolled to the side. Without even thinking, Dr. Lambro brushed his hand across the tabletop and tossed the remnants of his supper to the floor. "Put him down here," he said. "Quickly." He was already opening up the cape that had been wrapped about the boy. There was blood everywhere. The veins bulged from the boy's neck and his skin had turned a bluish pallor. *Cyanosis,* the doctor thought. *Traumatic tension pneumothorax, probably. Or worse.* "What happened?" he asked.

Colonel Maxwell was an imposing man, with a mighty barrel chest and massive head crowned with a thick gray mane of hair matted down by the inclement weather. He wore a brown frock coat, a mustard-colored waistcoat, and a cinder neckcloth over his white shirt. Never one for style, Maxwell still sported the muttonchops so popular among the military of the late Regency. Without turning, he hooked a thumb across one shoulder and said, "Struck by his lordship's landau on the London road. This is Dr. Lambro. The Marquess of Stanton and . . . companion."

Dr. Lambro looked up for but a second before continuing his work. The fat man with the round flat face had already stepped into the kitchen. He was obviously a dandy. Beneath his coat and cutaway, he wore a checkered sea blue waistcoat, and his neckcloth was tied so tightly that it braced his collar up against his ears. "You do me honor, your lordship. Please. Come in," said Dr. Lambro, trying to concentrate. Then he turned to Colonel Maxwell and added, "Pass me that knife there, by the sink. Be quick, man."

Colonel Maxwell did as he was told. Dr. Lambro took the blade. With care, he began to cut away the waistcoat and tattered, mud-stained shirt that clung like a second skin to the boy's chest.

"Heaven's above," the lady cried.

Two ribs stuck out of the boy's chest. As soon as Dr. Lambro had peeled away the clothing, a stream of blood began to seep out of the open wound. "It's as I feared. A lung's collapsed."

"I told you, darling, this was just a waste of time," the marquess said. "We're very late."

"Perhaps if you had brought him earlier . . ."

"That isn't what I meant," the marquess interrupted peevishly. "For our engagement."

"Your what?" Dr. Lambro looked up with surprise.

"We're to dine with the Earl of Leicester. Do not fret, good doctor—I'll pay you for your time. And the boy is obviously a vagabond. He shouldn't have been gamboling out there on the road."

Dr. Lambro's face grew white. His back arched visibly. "I would urge you, sir, to leave my house."

"What's that? What did you say?"

"I said get out. Get out of my house, right now."

"How dare you speak to me that way, with such impertinence," the marquess sputtered. "You forget your place, sir. I am a peer."

Dr. Lambro rushed against the marquess with the ferocity of a feral cat. He pushed his lordship up against the wall, grabbing his cutaway in his bloody hands. He brought his face up close and said, "I wouldn't care if you were king. Get out." He began to drag him toward the door. "Mark me, I say, or it will be you upon my table needing surgery."

"I would pay heed, your lordship," said the colonel, "if I were you. I know the doctor, and he is not a man to trifle with."

The marquess looked helplessly about the room. The coachman stayed his ground outside. The lady sidled toward the door. With a great effort, the marquess pulled himself away. His gray eyes bulged. His face grew red. He looked down at his bloody waistcoat. "Very well," he said, brushing his clothes. "We are already late. Besides, it smells in here of cabbage and the poor." Then, without another word, he turned and headed out the door.

Dr. Lambro stepped back to the table. He picked up the knife, placed the tip above the boy's third rib, and began to push the blade into the skin.

"Good God!" said Colonel Maxwell. "What are you doing, man?"

"Air is filling the cavity between the chest and lung. I need to relieve the pressure. Fetch me that pheasant."

Colonel Maxwell turned. A large cock dangled from the ceiling, tethered by its legs to bleed. He tore it loose and brought it over to the doctor.

Dr. Lambro plucked a quill out without ceremony, broke off both ends, and carefully removed the barbs. Then, with precision, he slipped the strawlike barrel down into the opening, immediately beside the blade. Next, he removed the knife. There was a small whistling sound as air began to leak out of the barrel of the plume. "Please, Colonel, shut the door."

The colonel stared for a moment at the three figures retreating down the garden path through the rain, bathed by the amber glow of the coachman's lantern. He closed the door and said, "By thunder, Lambro, you are a game one. To treat a peer with such contempt." A small smile played upon his lips. "Have you no fear?"

"I fear this boy will die if I don't operate immediately. And even then . . ."

"I've heard of the Marquess of Stanton. He'll not suffer this insult without satisfaction. You may count on that, sir."

"'Tis but his pride that's wounded. Look at this boy."

"But to make an enemy of Stanton . . . This boy's no kin to you."

In all his years of military service, Colonel Maxwell had weathered countless enemy barrages, had faced down hundreds of cavalry charges, thousands of anxious blades and bayonets.

And yet . . . there was something about the way the doctor glanced up from the table that made the blood freeze in his veins. Lambro seemed a man possessed.

The doctor smiled an icy smile and said, "No kin to me, perhaps; that's true." Then he looked down at the wounded boy and said, "But he's no stranger, Colonel Maxwell. I knew another boy once. Just like him. A long, long time ago. Another lifetime, really."

"Who was that?"

"Fetch me my surgeon's kit from the front room. Assist me, Colonel, if you would, and I will tell you."

PART I

·CHAPTER· I

FALL CAME EARLY, said Dr. Lambro, in the year of our Lord, 1830. In the city of Modena, on the south side of the Po Valley, the trees had already turned and leaves blew lazily about the cobblestone piazzas. They flew across the terra-cotta roofs, the bulbous domes of countless churches, pink and periwinkle walls, maelstroming upward, skyward to the apex of the duomo. Flanked in white marble, virgin of stone, the cathedral stood above the fray, atop the busy streets and thoroughfares, the frantic scurrying of man. . . .

In an abandoned lot nearby, a boy named Victor clambered through the rubble. Though only twelve years old, he was tall and thin, with striking hazel eyes, and hair the color of crows. He was dressed in dirty pantaloons, an off-white shirt, and his trademark tricolor hat—red, white, and green—a gift from his father, Roberto.

Victor had been out since early morning. He had traveled east from his parents' unassuming house off the Via San

Cristoforo, then north along the Corso Canalgrande toward the gardens of the Duke's estates. His mother, Catarina, was fond of flowers, and she had passed her passion on to Victor. He made the same journey almost every morning. The scents of the city smelled sweetest at dawn, before the heat of the day had evaporated them away: freshly baked loaves of bread from the ubiquitous bakeries and sweet shops that overflowed into the streets; fine herbs and flowers from the open-air markets of the piazzas; even fish brought in from the Panaro, the local river, or carried by cart from the distant Mediterranean Sea.

By the time Victor got to the Duke of Este's gardens, it was almost eight o'clock. A bell tolled, followed by another, and another, until they lifted up the morning, crisscrossing the city like cobweb threads, the strings of Pulcinella puppets, rising air light into the pitiless blue sky. Somewhere a rooster cried. Fall had come early, and with it that haunting autumn light which he so loved, cutting in at an angle and blanching the rose and cobalt walls, the lavender and pale green wooden shutters, the marble balconies and baked mud tiles of every villa of Modena.

The city held few secrets from the boy. Victor was an explorer by nature. At one point or another, he had ventured horizontally through every alleyway and *rua*—and vertically through time. Like the mice that burrowed through his basement's dank foundation, Victor was fond of digging. He had found black Etruscan vases off the Via Vignolese; silver *denari* stamped with the face of Emperor Septimius beneath the Chiesa di San Pietro, where the temple of Jupiter had once stood; and beads of twelfth century sea-blue glass, molded by artisans of the free commune.

Victor hesitated at the line of trees across the street from the gardens. He dipped his body, took a breath, and ran— fast as the wind—long legs reaching, cheetahlike, pouncing across the open ground and to the fence. He tossed himself to the ground. He could run fast. That much was certain. That much was sure. The gangs of the streets might curse his name, threaten his life, condemn him as a Carbonari, but he would always outrun them. He ran like Mercury. This notion came to him as he crawled through the dirt, and he banished it immediately as hubris. "Pride feeds no child," his father often said. He slipped under the fence. Vast flower beds stretched out before him in every direction, filled with bright scarlet amaryllis; *Cortusa matthioli*—long since withered—with their winsome serrated leaves; and his favorite, *Dictamnus albus*, Burning Bush. Careful to keep an eye out for the guards, he crept up to the *albus* and started digging at the roots. A strong scent, not unlike lemon peel, emerged as he worked the soil.

About two feet high, bearing spikes of fuchsia flowers, the plant bore an essential oil which exuded a vapor so powerful that passersby were warned not to come too close while carrying candles. His mother home-brewed remedies from the roots reputed to combat ailments of the nerves.

"Victor!"

He turned. He tucked his hat into his pants. He stowed his sack, half-filled with roots, into his off-white shirt. It was his neighbor Luciano. They called him the "fat rat" because, from certain angles, he looked precisely like one. He was lying on his stomach, his head wedged underneath the fence, peering in with doleful coal-black eyes. "Come quick," he said.

"What's the matter?" Victor had never seen Luciano quite so agitated.

"The Duke's Tyroleans. There was a fight. A man was killed and . . ."

"And? And what?"

"Your father's been arrested."

There were three of them, Tyroleans, Austrian Jaegers, dressed in light gray uniforms, golden buttons, green collars and cuffs, with jaunty dark brown hats curled up along one brim. They carried packs topped with gray blankets. They carried guns and swords.

One soldier was holding Victor's mother from the back, grasping Catarina by the elbow joints. She was straining to get away, to get to Victor's father, who was being held down by two other men. Roberto was lying on his stomach in the street. They were trying to bind his arms.

Raised from the Tyrolean mountain people, the soldiers were experienced hunters and marksmen. The one that Victor guessed must be the senior officer stood up and kicked his father in the face. Roberto groaned. Catarina broke free but was immediately overtaken by the third soldier. He threw her backward to the wall. She spat and faced him. She took a step, then two, when Victor heard the shot. It seemed unnaturally loud. His mother fell onto her knees, her arms outstretched, still reaching. She tumbled to the street without a sound. Victor ran up to her. He knelt down at her side. Blood gushed out of the open wound. He pressed his hand against her stomach, trying in vain to stem the flow. The blood was so red, so vivid and alive, that it transformed itself into a color, an abstract form, an intangible idea.

The Tyrolean stepped up, his gun still smoking. Victor could see his father. Roberto lifted himself up out of the street, a Jaeger still clinging to his back. His father shook him off. He turned. He faced the senior officer. Victor noticed that the officer had a bushy black mustache. He saw him lift his sword, and bring it down, and slice a gash across his father's upper chest. Roberto screamed but nothing seemed to come. But the blood. It poured out of his mouth and nose, out of the living wound. Roberto fell. Blood cartwheeled as he rolled across the ground.

Victor looked down at his dead mother. Her face seemed perfectly at peace now. The boy lifted his hand. He touched the rosy aperture of the wound, the lighter membrane of the large intestine, the stomach lining and the muscles and the paltry epidermis—so thin a covering, over so much. So thin!

"Who are you, boy?" one of the soldiers said, grabbing him by the shoulder.

"My name is Victor. This is my mother."

"What will we do with him?" another soldier said.

The senior officer began to wipe his sword across Roberto's back, cleaning the blade.

"We should kill him, too," said the soldier who had shot his mother. "Before he grows up to be another Carbonari."

Victor pressed his hand against his mother's wound. The blood; it wouldn't stop. She was dead but it kept coming.

"You know what that means, don't you, Victor?" The soldier spat his name out like a curse. "You know Ciro Menotti. You're a traitor to the Church, just like your father was."

Victor hung his head. Attendance at the secret meetings of the Carbonari marked you for death with the authorities. The Duke, supported by the Hapsburgs and the Pope, was trying to cleanse the land of revolutionaries like Menotti, who fought for a united Italy. But the world was growing up. The days of independent states, of petty fiefdoms juggled by the Holy See, were drawing to an end. New countries were being shaped by revolutions nearly every other month, throughout much of western Europe. The middle classes were questioning the divine rights of their kings. War was approaching, like a dim mist on the horizon. Like a plague.

"Don't kill him," the senior officer said.

Victor sat on the cobblestone street. *Like a cloud of locusts,* he thought.

He looked at his mother's face and wondered why the eyes and mouth and nose, the lines and creases he had grown to worship so devoutly, to love so absolutely over the years, now seemed so pointless and banal, so far away, and so less interesting than the roots of flesh which dangled from her stomach.

"I know a man in Genoa," the senior officer said, standing up. He slipped his sword back in his scabbard. A white gash opened up along his face, beneath his bushy black mustache. He was smiling. He was grinning as he said, "For a boy such as this, he'll pay plenty."

·CHAPTER·
2

THE *CERES* LAY AT HARBOR, flanked by two other merchant ships. Commonly called Pinks, from the Italian word *pinco*, the ship was relatively small, with a narrow stern, and rather slow to handle, given her square rigging. The crew of the *Ceres* found the appellation *pinco* ironically appropriate. *Pinco* not only means merchant ship in Italian; it's used to denote a person of little importance. Indeed, the *Ceres* was treated as a poor relation by the Rubattino shipping company, like a rather boring distant cousin. For unlike the massive spice ships which Rubattino dispatched to the Indies, the *Ceres* plied the waters off the western Mediterranean and Atlantic coasts. Mastering a Pink meant your career was going nowhere.

To add insult to injury, the crew of the *Ceres* often referred to the ship as the *Dimentico Demeter*, Demeter being the Greek equivalent of the Roman Ceres, Goddess of Agriculture, because they felt *dimentico* or "forgotten" by the principals of Rubattino.

The chief mate of the *Ceres*, Antonio Fabrizzio, was in the midst of considering his status in the world when the Tyrolean Jaeger entered the office of the shipping company, dragging a boy in his wake. That very morning, Fabrizzio had had another fight with his new wife, Angelina, about his meager salary, and he was not in a particularly good mood.

Fabrizzio was a small man with an egglike head, devoid of hair; a beaklike nose; and tiny dark brown eyes, the color of burned gravy. He knew the Tyrolean soldier; he had purchased crews from him before. "Roland. What a surprise," he said in a disengaged voice. "What brings you here? The *Ceres* is about to set sail. I'm very busy."

The Tyrolean soldier pushed the boy forward. Fabrizzio eyed him with suspicion. He was a good-looking lad with jet-black hair and striking hazel eyes. He looked about fourteen, perhaps younger. The boy stared back at him without a trace of fear. He seemed to linger in another world.

"Another boy. From Modena, this time," said the soldier. "See for yourself. He's strong and obedient. What say you, Antonio?"

"Modena is a landlocked piece of dung," Fabrizzio shot back. "Why do you always bring me boys with no experience?" He shook his head. "And the boy looks rheumy. Look at his eyes."

"Don't try to cheat me, Antonio. Examine his teeth. His arms and legs are strong. And he runs fast as the wind."

Fabrizzio laughed. "Where can one run on a Pink?" He stepped around the counter. He grabbed the boy by the hair, yanked his head back, and opened his mouth. The teeth appeared sound enough. In Fabrizzio's experience, teeth were a telltale sign. As the teeth crumbled, so did the bones. "What's your name, boy?"

"Victor."

Fabrizzio smiled halfheartedly. "Not so victorious, are we? Or we wouldn't be here." Fabrizzio poked and prodded Victor with his small, clawlike hands. "Where are your parents, Victor?"

"Dead. Both dead."

"How?"

Victor turned and pointed at the Austrian soldier. "He and the other Jaegers killed them."

The soldier frowned. He pulled at his mustache. "Carbonari. Both of them," he said.

Fabrizzio nodded. He stared out of the window at the distant harbor below. Several dozen ships lay at anchor beyond the long stone jetties. Most were Pinks, small and flat-bottomed, with narrow sterns. A few barges. A sprinkling of local sloops. But some were destined for the Indies, and they lay fat and heavy in the water, wide at the beam, laden with goods, waiting for the evening tide. "You have the luck of a gypsy, Roland," he said. "As it turns out, the *Ceres* is in need of a cabin boy."

"What happened to Alfonso?"

"Dead. Drowned off the coast of Spain last week. Tried to jump ship."

"You'll not be having any trouble from this one. He'll make a perfect cabin boy." The soldier grinned.

"How can you be so sure?"

"He's from Modena."

"And?"

"It's as you said. A landlocked turd. He cannot swim."

Victor couldn't sleep. Ever since leaving Modena, he found the nights most difficult. To sleep meant dreams. And dreams . . . Well, he preferred the stark truth of his wakeful life aboard the *Ceres*.

It was simple enough. He rose in darkness at the second bell, climbed to the galley, and prepared a cup of cider for the chief mate and two drams of rum for Captain Tarantino. Chief Mate Fabrizzio usually joined him by the third bell, at half past five, and they rocked about the galley silently, still half asleep. By the fourth bell everyone else was stirring, save for those who'd suffered through the dog watch. Victor brought the captain his rum. The men scampered through the rigging, unfurling sail, taking advantage of the morning breeze, as the sun crawled over the horizon. Victor helped Cookie get the morning meal together—hardtack and knots of pink pork knuckle from the night before.

Most of the men ate their breakfast in the rigging. It was Victor's job to carry the food aloft, in a large wooden bucket, lashed to his chest by a rope. He had grown used to the dizzying heights of the ship's mainmast. His long, strong legs bore him aloft like a monkey through the tangle of lines to the mizzen. At least for the first few weeks of the voyage. Before the storm off St. Malo. Before the accident.

They had been at sea for twenty-two days when it happened. They'd made their casual way along the northern Mediterranean coast: past Monte Carlo, Nice, Marseilles; down the coast of Spain, by Barcelona, Valencia, and Malaga; through the dizzying Strait of Gibraltar, the Gulf of Cadiz; past Lisbon and Porto in Portugal; and east to Vigo in Galicia, across the Bay of Biscay to the coast of France. After a while, the various ports began to blend together in Victor's mind. He was never granted shore leave. Despite their multifarious languages, their varying architecture and motley styles of dress, the towns and villages he watched slip past the starboard beam each day amalgamated into something simply foreign, and unattainable. Always an anchor cable distant. Just over there.

On this particular morning, the sea roiled and churned, black as oil. The first bell tolled, and Victor woke to the movement of Luigi at his ear. His pet mouse was hungry; he could tell. Luigi was making those plaintive squeaks to which Victor had grown accustomed, ever since finding him that first morning at sea in a crateful of pinafores in the Number 2 hold. Luigi was black with black eyes, save for that little patch of snowy white fur on his shoulder—shaped like a Lombard shield. Victor reached out for him but Luigi scampered away, along the hammock head, along the rope that held the bedding fast and aloft. "Come back here," Victor cried. The mouse ran down the bulkhead to the deck. He scurried through the door. With a breathless groan, Victor rolled over and tumbled from his hammock, giving chase.

He made his way along the corridor, and up the steps into the galley. Luigi was already waiting for him on the counter. He was standing on his hind legs, sniffing the air. Victor was about to chide him when he heard the sound of footsteps echoing behind him, just down the hall. *Strange,* thought the boy. It was still early; Cookie and the mate wouldn't be along for at least another hour. For some unfathomable reason, Victor ducked behind the counter. He waited out of sight. He waited until he felt the presence of the stranger entering the room.

Victor couldn't see him, but he could hear the seaman's footsteps as he made his way across the galley. The pantry door swung open. Then, nothing. Victor could not restrain himself. He poked his head out, around the corner, took a peek. A tall mariner, a Roman named Rubicon—with delicate brown eyes, a long, distinguished nose, and wispy black beard—stood by the open pantry door. He held an apple and some hardtack in one hand and a hunk of meat in the other. He was looking over his shoulder, staring at the galley door. Then he turned toward Victor.

Victor pulled back. He scurried underneath the counter, took a deep breath. Nothing happened. Not a sound, save for the juicy snap of Rubicon chomping his apple. Then, without warning, the mariner started to move toward the counter. Victor pressed his back against the panel immediately below the countertop. He froze. The seaman took another step, then hesitated. Victor could hear him close the pantry door. He made his way across the galley, stopped for a moment by the counter, just for a second, and then headed out the door. He was gone. Victor glanced around the counter. The galley was empty. The Roman mariner was shuffling down the corridor, heading belowdecks toward the sleeping quarters.

Victor told no one about the incident, but it didn't take long for Cookie to uncover the theft. He had an uncanny ability to calculate the measure of food. He could tell the difference between a pound of flour and a pound minus two teaspoons. His eye was acute. Thus, the missing hardtack led to the pilfered apple, and the apple to the pork knuckle. Cookie had been at sea for more than fifteen years. He knew the combinations men favored. He raised the alarm to the chief mate, who put the word out to the crew, and finally—and with reluctance—Victor himself was summoned to the captain's quarters.

"Cabin boy," Chief Mate Fabrizzio said. He seldom called Victor by name.

"Yes, sir." Victor hovered just outside the captain's fo'c'sle, on the lip of the cabin door.

"Don't just stand there," said Fabrizzio. "Come in. Come in."

Victor did as he was told. The captain's quarters seemed the stuff of royalty. The master of the merchant ship *Ceres* had handsome silk bedspreads, Phoenician purple, embroidered with a pair of interlocking dragons. Colorful charts festooned the walls, sprinkled with sea monsters. A silver tea service sat by the window; beside it a mahogany chest, hand-carved from a solitary tree from Sumatra. The captain sat at his table, staring out the window. A real window, not a porthole. A real window with muntins of lead.

Captain Tarantino was unnaturally tall, with a rather small head on a very long neck. His languorous eyes were nut brown. His eyebrows arched together in a point. He seemed sempiternally taxed, overburdened, for his tall, impressive forehead was always resplendent with sweat. Captain Tarantino glowed, no matter what the temperature. He looked, to Victor, to be perpetually suffering from fever.

"Sit down," said the captain. He pointed at the only empty chair beside him. The others were already occupied by Cookie and the mate. Victor sat.

"We have heard it said," Fabrizzio suddenly exclaimed, "on good account, that you were awake this morning early. At first bell."

"I was?"

"You were seen by several seamen stealing from your hammock, running after that pet mouse of yours. You went into the galley, in hot pursuit, following your vermin. Is this not so?"

"Yes, sir." Victor looked about. Captain Tarantino was staring off at nothing in particular. He was holding a white kerchief, scented with lavender, to his nose. His fingers were as delicate as quills.

Cookie, with his bald pate and beady blue eyes, seemed to be following an insect through the air. His eyes rolled about in their sockets. His swollen fingers, fat as baby sausages, tapped the surface of the table. He was anxious to conclude the affair.

And Chief Mate Fabrizzio, with his egglike head and tiny dark brown eyes, the color of burned gravy, he just kept pecking at Victor. "And did you not, cabin boy, then steal into the pantry, into the very heart of the ship's stores, and purloin several articles of food?"

"I didn't steal anything."

"Come, sir," said Captain Tarantino. "Get on with it. We know who took the food."

"Being thorough, Captain. Simply being thorough. We don't yet fully know the boy's role in the incident, his level of involvement, that sort of thing." The chief mate sat up. He stared at Victor down his nose. "What did you see?" he added, trying to smile. "Or, more precisely, who?"

"What do you mean, sir?"

"You know exactly what I mean. Who did you see in the pantry? Who took the food?"

"I don't know, sir."

"Don't trifle with me, boy. If you're dishonest, I'll hold you guilty as the thief himself. And it will not go easy on him. That, I assure you. Now, who was he? Answer me. I said, answer me." He shook Victor by the arm. "Answer me. Answer me, damn you."

"Oh, for God's sake," Captain Tarantino said. He leaned across the dining table. "You're scaring the boy half to death. It was Rubicon, wasn't it?" he said. "Wasn't it?" He rubbed his long nose. He waved his handkerchief and smiled. "We know he took that food. We found pork knuckles in his kit. Tell me, boy. It was Rubicon, wasn't it? Wasn't it?"

Victor nodded.

"There," said Captain Tarantino. "Doesn't it make you feel better—telling the truth?"

Victor shook his head. "No, sir. Not really."

They made the entire crew witness Rubicon's flogging. It was not the first punishment Victor had seen meted out aboard the *Ceres*. Chief Mate Fabrizzio ran a tight ship. "Don't spare the rod," he was fond of saying. And he didn't.

This time, however, it was special. This time they used a cat-o'-nine-tails. Each thong was fitted with a pointed stone, and when they flogged him, it opened up great gashes in his back. Rubicon began to bleed. Badly. Blood coursed across the deck, pitched as the Pink rolled. Victor was forced to watch as the seaman gradually disintegrated. At first, Rubicon had been stalwart, even proud. At the beginning, he'd refused to even touch the mast to which his wrists were bound. But after only a few lashings, he began to lean against the oaken spar, to recline upon it, until—by the twelfth or thirteenth stroke—Rubicon was dangling from the rusty iron bracelets. He hung there like a chrysalis, oblivious of the other world around him, clinging to his pain.

They brought him down, finally, released him. He lay there for a moment as they rinsed his bloody wrists. He lay there, looking up with his sad eyes, his long, distinguished nose, now battered, his wispy blood-flecked beard. He lay there, quietly, simply looking up at Victor. He kept on staring even as they turned him over, even as they held him down and dumped a bucketful of black seawater on his back.

·CHAPTER· 3

SEPTEMBER, 1830

THE ENGLISH CHANNEL

IN HIS THREE LONG WEEKS aboard the *Ceres,* Victor thought that he had witnessed all the faces of the sea. He had admired turquoise pools off Monaco, tide-sculpted coral outcroppings off the coast of France, mysterious grottoes scooped from the cliffs of Spain. He'd seen the warm and rich blue waters of the Mediterranean commingle with the inky tendrils of the ocean at Gibraltar. He'd seen squalls and days of torpor, when the sea fell flat as glass, and the far horizon grew bewildered in the mist. He'd seen cloudless skies and stormy weather, whitecaps and rollers. Off Portugal, he'd spent three hours studying whales.

Victor had never been aboard a ship before the *Ceres,* at least not one of any size. The rowboats and single-masted sloops which plied the waters of the slithering Panaro didn't count. It could be said, though, that the magic of a fourteen-hundred-ton East Indiaman was hidden in the meanest cutter. No matter what the vessel's size, all sailing was essentially the same. In truth, one could reduce the most complicated vessel to its most elemental parts—just like the human body.

At the basis of all rigging was the mast, whether constructed out of one or many pieces. Fixed to the deck like a backbone through the human body, the mast was secured and controlled by ropes, the so-called "standing rigging." Despite the name, most masts were made of different parts, including topmast and topgallant mast, and these subcomponents could be, and were often, lowered. *Standing* was a relative term. Masts, including the bowsprit at the front, supported the sails. Sails were the muscles of the ship, flexed by the wind. They covered the skeletal masts. They were everywhere, blocking each passage of even the most feeble breeze across the ship's hard casing. They hung from the yards, spars slung to the masts themselves; from gaffs, on spars projecting from the masts; or traveled back and forth on ropes called stays, such as the jibs suspended by halyards from the foremast to the bowsprit.

The entire network of ropes by which the booms, yards, and sails were manipulated comprised the "running rigging"—so called because the lines were constantly in use, heaved to trim yards, to make or shorten sail. They also provided the crew with a means to travel aloft. Shrouds, threaded with ratlines, were pressed into service as rope ladders. Victor had climbed to every part of the vessel, from the tops at the head of the masts, past the crosstrees and topgallant shrouds, to the fore-truck at the pinnacle of the foremast. He'd learned to scurry along horses—footropes which dangled two to three feet under each spar, extending from the middle of the yards across each arm. Victor was fearless, and the seamen grew to admire him. In only three weeks he climbed the rigging with the same speed and dexterity as the best of them. And he often did it laden with grub, with bolts of sailcloth, or with several turns of line.

But he was not prepared for the storm that gathered off the coast of Brittany. It was barely two o'clock, and already the sky was dark—and still. One minute the wind had been busy stoking whitecaps; the next it was gone. Simply gone. Victor watched as every seaman stopped and turned and stared across the gunwales at the sea. A lime-green creamy light descended on the deck. The water flattened out, as if pressed by some gigantic unseen hand. Seabirds began to circle slowly overhead. The captain suddenly appeared on deck. It was as if he'd felt it, too. The stillness choked the breath out of one's very chest.

Captain Tarantino scanned the distant coast of Brittany. "We won't make harbor," he said almost apologetically. He looked down at Fabrizzio. "Quick now, Chief Mate. Before it's in our laps. Make as much sheet as she'll handle. To windward."

The chief mate scurried down the mast house steps across the deck. "Close hauled!" he yelled. "Look lively there."

The men began to make sail. Then, as if on cue, the wind reappeared. The men started a dance of delicate balance, making and trimming sail as the vessel tacked seaward, fighting the wind. When they had rounded the headland, the northern breezes picked up, filling the courses and topsails. Sailcloth snapped and the ship picked up speed. Men scurried about, hauling on hawsers, toting line. Victor could hear the main and foremasts complain. The rigging was feeling the pressure as the *Ceres* plunged—head and stern—through the troughs of the waves.

"Cabin boy. You there. Victor!"

It was the chief mate. He was standing immediately behind Victor. In the shrill noise of the wind and the constant pitching of the deck, Victor hadn't noticed him approach. "Yes, sir," the boy said.

"Get below and tend to Rubicon. He's screaming like a hound from hell."

"Me, sir?"

"Am I staring at another? I entrust his health to you, boy. Don't disappoint me."

Victor squatted down to meet another breaker. Water washed in, crashing through scuppers. Dark flinty tides tugged at his feet. "Aye, sir," he said.

It took him several minutes in the pitching seas to make it to the sleeping quarters. The lower decks seemed strangely quiet now, eerily empty, after the chaos of the rigging. Victor found it difficult to negotiate the stairs. Each time the ship rolled, the steps rose up to greet him, like a drawbridge, until they stood straight up, quite perpendicular, a solid wall of steps. And then that pause of anxious expectation. And then the steps reclined, like some appeasement gesture, backed off and down, until they lay completely flat.

"Who's that?" said Rubicon as Victor gradually approached.

"It's me. Victor."

Rubicon turned in his hammock. He winced in pain. Victor could see his eyes roll in his head. "Get away from me. I'll cut you. So help me God, I will."

Victor stopped for a moment by his hammock and removed a small sack from the kit at his feet. It was his bag of albus roots. "The chief mate ordered me below. He told me to look after you," he said. He made his way between the other hammocks to the corner of the fo'c'sle where Rubicon was dangling from the ceiling. The ship pitched and Victor had to hold on to prevent himself from slipping. The Roman mariner looked pale, white as sea froth. He lay on his side, his back exposed to the air. Victor began to squeeze the roots in his hands, milking them of their clear pungent liquid. After a few moments, he stepped behind Rubicon. "This may sting in the beginning," he said. Without waiting for an answer, he applied the sticky liquid to the wounds.

Rubicon shuddered. He tried to pull away, but there was nowhere he could go. He was trapped in his hammock like a fly in a web. He squirmed and moaned as the boy applied the salve. "It wasn't enough to see me flogged," the Roman seaman said. "You have to rub salt in my wounds."

"It will stop the pain. Give it a moment. You'll feel better."

The seaman spun about. He fastened Victor by the neck. He drew him close. "There's but one thing that will make me feel better . . . and that's to watch you squirm." He reached down, down, with his free hand, down to where no hand should go, and wrapped his fingers around flesh. Victor tried to wriggle free but Rubicon held him tight. He couldn't move. He couldn't get away. He felt the seaman squeeze and say, "I should gut you right here. Right now, boy. But I don't have my knife, more's the pity." He twisted his wrist. He wrenched, then relaxed. He fondled what he had squeezed. His fingers stroked bare skin. "My mother used to say, 'Don't eat all your pie in one sitting.'" He patted Victor like a dog. "I should be patient. Bide my time. You're a pretty boy, and we've a long journey ahead of us."

Victor saw his opportunity. He tore himself free, stepped back, out of reach. He suddenly felt nauseous.

Rubicon tried to grab him. Victor jumped back. He took another step, then stopped. He looked down at Rubicon, noticed his smile, the way it curled up in the corner, noticed his talonlike hands. Without warning, Victor punched Rubicon in the face. Once. Twice. Three times. In rapid succession. Until Rubicon roared. He rolled onto his feet. Despite his livid wounds, he staggered after Victor, who was already half-way up the stairs.

Rubicon chased the boy topside. Victor sprinted out into the rain. The boards were awash with inky waters and he almost lost his footing several times before he threw himself into the shroud. He wormed his way aloft, ratline to ratline. Rubicon followed close behind. The Roman mariner almost ran into the chief mate, who told him to "stand down," but Rubicon ignored him. He leaped into the rigging. He paid no attention to the wind and rain, the pitching of the vessel, the fact that all the hawsers in the ship had been got up to mastheads, and hence hove taut; that way the ship could bear more sail. He didn't give a fig about the captain's desperate measures to outrun the storm. His only care was of the skinny cabin boy who scurried up the lines before him, only a few feet distant. Straight ahead. Just out of reach.

Victor climbed and climbed, from the mainmast top to the mizzen stay, from mizzen topmast to the topgallant. From line to sail to line, they charged. The mainmast swung and shook, pitching first forward as the ship slipped through another trough, then to the side as the vessel cut cross-breeze. Victor was blinded by the rain. He looked down. Rubicon was getting closer. He could see the seaman climbing with a grim determination. The wounds on his back had reopened. They fluttered like ribbons of skin. They flapped in the wind. Rubicon's eyes seemed to glow from some strange inside light. He drew closer and closer. Victor looked up. The ship rolled, shook, and shuddered. Victor lost his footing then. His hand simply dislodged. He cried out, but his scream was stolen by the wind. No one could hear him as he gradually unrolled, right there, midair, as he fell and flattened out, just as the deck rose up to greet him. The crash was so loud that it vanished. One minute it filled his consciousness; then it was gone, replaced by a grim tearing sound, a click, a snap. Victor looked up and the lime-green light enveloped him, like Saint Elmo's fire on the topsail-braces, wrapped him up in the knowledge that he was still alive, but that his leg, for some unexplained reason, was dead . . . and always would be. The pain came afterward. It burst throughout his body like a blast of morning light, like a spring shower, filled every crevice of his being, from the very deepest rift to the shallowest depression, with omnipresent anguish. He screamed. Blood rushed into his head. It sang inside him. It sang with the unbridled grace of every race that he had ever won, and with the speed of every victory. It howled and everything went black.

He runs fast as the wind. . . .
Where can one run on a Pink?
He runs. . . .
Where?

When he came to, Victor was still lying on the deck. The chief mate and captain hovered over him, their heads together, looking down. He tried to speak, but the words wouldn't settle within him. They scrambled like lobsters in the cave of his heart. Victor glanced down. He saw what used to be his leg. It was shattered. He could not count the pieces. It wriggled as the planks pitched. Sackful of bones. Casing of gristle. It rolled and writhed on the deck.

"He'll never walk again," said the chief mate. "What a damned nuisance. I'll have to amputate."

Just then Luigi scrambled out of Victor's pocket. The mouse had survived the fall. He dashed across the pitching deck. He ran, half-swam, to Rubicon. In a straight line. As if on purpose. Through the shadow of Rubicon's boot. There was a discernable crunch as the seaman put his foot down on the mouse. He twisted his boot for good measure. Two others grabbed Rubicon and pulled him away.

"I'll deal with you next," said Fabrizzio. The chief mate stepped up. "Count on it."

The captain brought his kerchief to his face. He rubbed the scent of lavender against his senses. "A cabin boy who cannot walk is of no value to this ship." He looked at Victor. "I'm sorry, but it can't be helped. You slipped. Can you hear me, boy? You slipped." He stared across the bulwarks at the sea. "Perhaps, whoever poses as God has other plans for you."

Victor tried to say something, but he couldn't find his voice. The air had been knocked out of him, forced from his chest. It was difficult to breathe.

The captain shook his head. "It pains me to see you like this, Victor," he said. "Throw him overboard."

They picked him up. Victor could feel that. He could feel his leg hanging free, ripping the tendons surrounding the knee. He screamed again. "Put me down," he shouted. "Put me down, please. I can walk."

The seamen hoisted him aloft. He saw the chief mate's face, his shiny head, that soft ridge of fine hair around his tonsure. He saw the deck swing around below, saw it replaced by frothing seas, saw each and every wave sweep by until the water slapped him. Hard. He tumbled wildly through the waves. They'd thrown him overboard! The ocean plunged through his nose and his mouth. He coughed, breathed in more water. He spun about. His legs flailed uselessly, his arms, his head. He kicked and heaved and came up out of the water, riding waves. He floundered in the whitecaps, aware that he was breathing, aware of stars and then that great flat panel of the deepest iridescent black, the port side of the vessel, as she shuddered quietly along, away, horizon bound. Hopelessly out of reach. Victor heard a distant splash. A moment later, a spar swam by. He barely saw it in the dark. He lunged upon it as it passed. He curled his body around the gaff. He hugged the rig, wondering, who had knocked it overboard? The captain or chief mate? One of the crew?

And more infuriating: why? It was far, far better to wonder at the meanest mystery than to feel the pain. Why had they even bothered? His leg was shattered. He could not swim. He was alone and helpless in the middle of the sea.

·CHAPTER·
4

SEPTEMBER, 1830
PORTSMOUTH, ENGLAND

PALE, PALE MOON. It stared, cold Cyclops eye. It sailed across the firmament, indifferent. A wound in the great blackness. A hole in the shade to let the morning in. The sun replaced the moon. It peered across the cut of the horizon, less indifferent than contemptuous; a great bronze platter to serve up his pain and thirst and endless solitude. He was a speck in the great wash of the Channel, as insignificant as sea lice on the flukes of whales. He clung relentlessly to his gaff. He suckled at the spar. He rose and fell and rose again, his shattered leg a lifeless rudder. He felt his tongue grow fat and thick and full of salt. He sweated and grew chill.

He had lost count of the long hours, of the long days of constant drifting. He had past caring of his fortune. He looked upon the gaff now as his enemy, for it prevented him from slipping down into the depths to sleep. But he could not bring himself to open up his fingers, to simply pull his hands away, let go. Try as he might to free himself, he was a prisoner of life.

By the end of the third day, he started seeing apparitions. At first they were extensions of his vision: The tops of waves began to bleed into the sky; the lip of the horizon rolled, like an old sea chart, drawing the edges of the world up into a bowl. It was filled with liquid agony. He tried to block the visions from his mind. He tried to think of other things. But they grew richer and more varied. They grew more reasonable, too. He started seeing people drifting next to him. Bodies of seaweed. Figures of flotsam. He saw his mother and his father float—just out of reach—along the current underneath his feet, imprisoned in green glass. His mother's stomach had become a nest for fish, haven for eels. His father's mostly severed arm gave up a momentary wave. As it passed by, it moved. Was it the current or a last farewell? Was it the fin of some leviathan? He felt his head begin to spin, to tip, just like the seabirds overhead. Just overhead, they wheeled and ducked and darted. They pointed him to shore.

His bloated leg plowed up the shingles of the beach. Victor was too tired to scream. He was too tired to feel the pain. He was too thirsty, too, he was. At least he was. He was!

A dog barked in his head. He heard him plainly. It was a dog. He felt his cold nose on his neck. He heard him sniffing. He tried to push the animal away but Victor could not raise his hand. His arm was locked around the spar. He felt the stones against his cheek. He heard the surf, the whistle, and the dog stepped back. A hand reached down. He felt it grab the collar of his shirt. He felt it drag him up the beach. He fell, and rolled, and looked up at a kind and wizened face.

The old man said something. Victor could hear his voice. He saw his pale blue eyes, his lips and snow-white hair. The man said something else but the words were strange. The anchor would not hold. The cable parted and the phrases drifted off. Into the breeze. Victor looked up, and smiled, and turned and vomited.

The dog began to lick the strand. The old man laughed, a sound so full and welcoming, so providential, that Victor felt himself curl up into a ball. He pulled the melody around him like a blanket. He tucked himself inside, and fell asleep.

The old man carried the boy home in his arms. He lived in a driftwood shack just off the beach, in a gully which sliced the nearby cliffs and ran progressively higher to the plains above. He tended to Victor's wounds, watched over him, praying that gangrene wouldn't set in. And for some reason it didn't, as if the briny seawater had somehow pickled the appendage, preventing it from decomposing.

The old man spoke no Italian, and Victor knew no English, yet they managed to communicate. Hand signals, gestures, expressions: These were their syntax. It was not difficult. There was only so much Victor needed while confined to his straw-filled crypt at the rear of the shack. And for most of the first week, he was delirious with fever anyway.

The old man lived by himself, save for his border collie, named Tatters. He tended a few dozen sheep that he kept on the meadow above. Or, more accurately, it was Tatters who tended the sheep. The old man spent most of his days simply roaming the strand, beachcombing for flotsam and jetsam. Victor guessed he was a smuggler of sorts, or a wrecker—one who lures ships ashore with bright lights, running them up on the rocks to be plundered. Victor couldn't be certain. One afternoon, several months after his rescue, he discovered a cellar at the rear of the shack half-filled with found cargo, destined never to be taxed by the realm. But, smuggler or no, the old man treated Victor with kindness. He fed him and helped him eliminate. He washed him and dressed him and cleaned up his vomit. He coddled him like a baby. And, indeed, that's exactly how Victor felt; helpless and alone, a stranger in a strange land.

Remarkably, in only a month or two, Victor began to heal. He even managed to hobble about a bit on a crutch which the old man had made out of driftwood. Victor thought it appropriate. He felt like driftwood himself: half carved, incomplete. It was as if a part of him had been lost during the storm, something that made him who he was. It floated there somewhere, still, out at sea. A derelict. Phantom limb. It lingered in the currents and the tides.

Over time, the boy grew to love the old man. And his dog. Tatters, at least, loved him back. Normally furious with strangers who ventured too proximate, the collie was oddly at peace around Victor. Perhaps because Victor was wounded, a nonthreat. Or because he was still just a boy. For the life of him, Victor didn't know why.

The old man himself was half lame. He had suffered some

injury long ago—judging from the great scar on his leg—and he spent most of his waking hours with a hand around a sheep's crook, hobbling about. Victor would watch him each morning from a hole in the hayloft, as he made his way up the ravine after breakfast, leading his sheep; they were penned in at night by the shack. An hour or so later, the old man would reappear on the path, picking his way through the rubble, hobbling along. He'd be sure to look in on his ward one more time, to be certain, then he'd head down the track to the beach. Hobbling and hobbling, searching for cargo.

Victor had been with the old man for almost two months before he even learned where he was. The old man lived near a city named Portsmouth. And it wasn't in France, but in something called Hampshire. Somehow or another, the storm had blown the *Ceres* halfway across the Channel, and Victor had drifted the rest, onto England. A whole other country.

The old man was called Peter Smith. Victor wondered if Smith were his real name, for the old man kept a large sea chest by his bed with the initials *PL* carved in the lid—not *PS*. After three months, Victor knew enough English to be able to ask him about it. But the old man was reluctant to talk. He put on an air of confusion. He just shook his head, turned away, and after a while Victor wearied and finally gave up. There were some things the old man didn't want to acknowledge. And that was just fine with the boy. Victor had his own secrets to nurture, his own painful memories. He kept them inside him, like a cavern of mushrooms. He tended them nightly while dreaming.

Time passed uneventfully. Victor grew stronger and stronger. The old man had set the leg with a series of sticks, which he'd tied with ingenious precision. Victor marveled at the knots. They were as intricate as any he had seen aboard the *Ceres*. Perhaps the old man had once been a mariner.

They hobbled together, the old man and the boy—the one with his sheep's crook, the other his crutch. They walked and they walked, hunting for objects of value: lost rope; kegs of oil or of wine; casks of rum; bales of cloth; all manner of things that the sea had thrown up on the beach.

When Victor grew tired, they'd sit on the strand, simply sit there in silence and stare at the sea, at the bright glistening waves of the Channel. Sometimes boats would pass by, usually sloops or small cutters. Sometimes larger ships. After a while, they'd continue down the beach, or return for their dinner at noon—a crust of bread and some cheese which the old man made himself from ewe's milk.

Usually, Victor stayed home after dinner, trying to rest. More often than not, he ended up fiddling about in the shack, mending net, tidying up. On occasion, he'd follow the path through the cleft to the meadow. He and Tatters would sit there together, watching over the flock. He would lie on his back and stare up at the clouds, wondering where they had come from and where they were going. Then as the sun set, he'd hobble with Tatters back home, picking his way through the boulders. He'd stop, every time, at the head of the path, and look down.

The view here was tranquil and warming. The way the shack looked, the snowy white smoke which poured out of the chimney like cream, the warm glow of oil lamps, the sounds of the old man inside, making supper; framed as it was by the sea, by the lavender sky, already dotted with stars, and with clouds drawing in from the south; set as it was in the twilight, Victor was overcome by a strange sense of peace. So much had happened since that fateful morning he'd run off to dig roots at the Duke of Este's estate in Modena. So much that was bad. Where was he to set this tranquility? It just didn't belong.

Then, one night, the daydreamy glow of their lives was blown out like a candle. Victor had been sleeping in the hayloft at the rear of the shack when he woke with a start. The old man was pressing a hand to his mouth.

"Shhh," hissed the old man. "Be still. We have visitors."

Victor could hear Tatters howling outside.

"Come," he continued.

They hobbled outdoors. Someone had opened the pen. The sheep were being led up the path.

The old man and Victor gave chase. After a while, they heard Tatters. One minute he was barking, and the next came a yelp. The collie cried out. Then again. Then he stopped. The old man glanced over at Victor. Victor could see the worry in his eyes, reflected in the moonlight.

They scrambled up the path, even faster now. Suddenly, Victor heard voices. Clouds swept from the moon and the path was revealed. Two men raced through the cleft. They were heading aloft, to the meadow. A pair of dogs, herding sheep, ran beside them. They were stealing them!

"Wait here," said the old man.

"But they're getting away."

"You're still wounded."

"No, I'm not," Victor said. "I feel mended. Hurry up, or we'll lose them for certain."

"I said wait," said the old man as he pulled the boy back by the collar. Then he was gone.

Clouds gathered like wolves around the moon. Victor could hear the sheep bleating in panic. He could hear the two dogs. They were growling and barking, and snapping their jaws. But Tatters was silent. He'd been killed, or run off. Victor couldn't be sure. He waited there quietly for a few moments more in the darkness, and then spat, "Oh, to blazes." He started again up the path. He climbed and he climbed when he felt a light wind touch his cheek, then the hard sudden impact of someone upon him. He spun to the ground. A shard of hot pain pierced his leg. His bad leg. The one bundled up in its own lobster trap of wood slats and gray webbing. He rolled and he rolled. The man vanished. The night was too black. The path was a tunnel of darkness. Victor tried to get up. He rolled to one knee, used his crutch as a lever. He started to rise when the man reappeared from the shadows. He snatched Victor's staff. Victor fell. The attack was so sudden that he didn't have a chance to prepare. Victor fell on his face in the dirt. He rolled, and looked up.

The stranger was barely visible in the dim moonlight. He was not that much older than Victor. A young man, to be sure. His hair was drawn back from his face, tied up with a ribbon. His sideburns were thin. He had a rather large nose, somewhat flat; small eyes; and a petulant mouth. He was holding the crutch. Victor's crutch. The stranger grinned as he brought it aloft, raised it high. Victor shielded his face with his hand, preparing to parry the blow, when he heard, and then noticed, the crook.

The old man came out of the night. Just as the stranger was dropping the crutch like an ax on Victor's head, the crook blocked the blow. There was a crack as the staves came together. The young man leaped back. Victor heard sheep bleat and the clouds rolled away. Waxy moonlight exploded around them, revealing the path and the other two men, and the dogs, and the sheep coursing skyward, along the ravine to the meadow. *Crack, crack.* The young man swung the crutch in a circle above him, around and around, trying to strike the old man in the head. But the old man ducked deftly. He twirled his sheep's crook through the air with such speed that the wood disappeared. Victor had never seen anything like it.

The old man stepped back, the crook on his shoulders. It was balanced precisely. He swung it aloft, and then down. It struck the young man on the head. The stranger retreated; he staggered and dropped to his knees.

The old man stepped up. The crook whistled, spun. He thrust the stave out like a spear. It struck the young man in the sternum. He grunted, collapsed, gasped for breath. The old man struck him again. The crook chipped his chin. The young man spun backward; he tumbled and fell.

The old man approached him with caution. Once again, he used the crook as his staff. He prodded the stranger with the tip of his boot.

The young man didn't stir. The old man examined him for a moment, then turned and looked up toward the meadow.

The other two strangers were no longer in sight. Nor were the sheep. They were getting away. "Here," said the old man. He kicked the crutch over to Victor. "If he rises again, put him down."

Victor watched as the old man hobbled up the cut in pursuit. Within seconds he had vanished around the bend at the top of the cliff. Victor glanced back at the stranger. He still lay on the ground, still unconscious. The blow had opened his chin; it was bleeding. There was a very large bump on his head. But, at least, Victor thought, he was breathing.

Just then, he heard a high, familiar whine. Victor turned. There! He got up. He hobbled over through the darkness. On the side of the path, half hidden by a bush, lay Tatters. Victor sat down by the ragged heap. The dog was still breathing. The boy ran his hand through the fur on his neck. He cradled his head in his hands. "Are you all right, boy?" he said. "Good boy. Good boy, Tatters." Victor noticed that the dog's right foreleg had been broken. There was blood in his ear, and a long shallow cut on his cheek. Then Victor spoke in Italian, for the first time in weeks. "You're just jealous," he said. "Want a crutch of your own." The sound of the words squeezed his heart. The dog didn't move. Victor patted him gently. "We'll be three cripples now on the beach. Just like us, boy; that's right. Like your master and me."

Stone scraped on stone right behind him. Victor turned just in time to catch the back of the young man who'd attacked him as he scarpered away down the path. Shingles scattered. He slipped and he fell, and he started again. Then he vanished, swallowed up by the shadows.

The old man reappeared on the path. He was herding a half dozen sheep. The rest, it appeared, had been lost. The whole flock. More than two dozen animals.

As he approached, the old man barely noticed the boy. There were tears in his eyes. Victor could see that. His face was bleached by the moonlight. "What happened? Did they get away?" Victor asked.

The old man nodded. "I lost them," he said. "I just couldn't keep up . . . with my leg. I couldn't keep up." The old man shook his head and knelt down on the path next to Tatters.

"He's alive," Victor said. "But his right leg is broken."

The old man was weeping. Victor noticed tears make their way through the maze of fine wrinkles that crisscrossed Smith's face. He'd been undone by the incident. His hands shook as he petted the dog. Then he stood. He looked up toward the meadow, as if to catch one final glimpse of the flock. He stared at the sky. He stood there, as if listening, his fingers clutching the crook. "Come on," he said, finally. "Help me lift Tatters. On your feet, boy."

"Why bother?" said Victor.

The old man stood perfectly still. "What did you say?"

"You heard me."

"Get up."

"Why? I'll be down here again soon enough." Victor stared at the dog. Without warning, he picked up his crutch and then tossed it aside. It slithered away, down the path.

The old man sighed. "Tell me, boy," he inquired. "Have you ever heard the riddle of the Sphinx?"

Victor ignored him. He watched Tatters as he breathed.

The dog was unconscious. He was still blissfully unaware of the world.

"Well, I'll tell you," the old man continued. "What walks on four legs in the morning, two legs at noon, and three in the evening?"

Victor ignored him at first. He kept patting the dog on the neck. Then he turned, with a scowl, and said, "I don't know. But I fancy you do, Mr. Smith. I give up."

"So I see," said the old man. He started to laugh. Without warning he struck Victor's crutch on one end with his crook. It bounced and he struck it again with a quick second thrust. Victor's staff spiraled upward and around, through the air, around and around. It landed right beside Victor.

Once again, the boy was surprised by the old man's command of the crook. Victor reached out and picked up his crutch. He stared at the wood in his hand. "How did you do that?" he asked.

"The answer to the riddle is Man," said the old man. "A baby crawls on all fours, a man walks on two. And when you get to be as old as I am, or when you're injured, this here," he said, shaking his crook, "your staff becomes your third leg."

Victor struggled to his feet. "Who taught you how to fight like that?" he said.

"Long ago, I was a seaman on a frigate. We sailed to Japan, to Malacca, the Indies. I met a Chinaman there, and he taught me."

Victor hobbled over beside him. "Will you teach me?"

The old man smiled. "A man with three legs is still a man, Victor. Never forget that. It's the natural state of things. It simply came to you early." He started peeling off his shirt. He knelt down on the path, right next to Tatters. He began to bind the animal's wounds with strips of cloth torn from his shirt. Tatters moaned, tried to stir.

"Hush, dog," he said.

"Well, will you?"

The old man didn't turn around. He just kept bandaging the dog. When he'd finished, he looked down at his handiwork, and said, "Yes, Victor. I will teach you."

·CHAPTER·
5

ANOTHER MONTH SLIPPED BY. It had been four months
since Victor's rescue from the sea, although he had no
way of knowing. The old man kept no clock or calendar. It
had grown cold and damp, a kind of weather to which Victor
was unused. It rained each afternoon, the clouds heavy and
black, and so close; almost at arm's length, precariously close;
an intangible comforter newly thrown on the earth. It was the
morning of Christmas Eve, and Victor had gone fishing.

He sat on a pyramid of rocks that jutted from the outside
edge of a small bay not far from Langstone Harbor. It had
been a good day so far: a few pouting; two bass—rather small—
and a dab; the first smoothhound of the year, a good twenty-
four inches. And, best of all, a large flounder. It was one of
the old man's favorite dishes, and, since the robbery, food had
been scarce. The fish would make a sumptuous Christmas Eve
supper.

Victor gathered up his gear. It was still early, but he didn't

want to press his luck. It looked as if it were going to pour
. . . again. He whistled and Tatters hobbled down the beach.
The dog's right foreleg was trussed up in a wicker sling. He
slithered and skipped through the sand.

They made their way along the beach, back toward the old
man's shack. Gray clouds rolled overhead. They hurled themselves on top of one another, like dogs in a pack. They swept
and eddied. The sea began to grow more turbulent. The wind
pitched up the waves. They crashed and splashed into the air
at times so high that it was difficult to know where they concluded and the clouds began.

By the time Victor could see the shack, he was exhausted.
Twice he had fallen, simply from fatigue. The flounder seemed
to have grown larger on the trek, as if its bladder had expanded.
It bounced and smacked against his leg. His rod felt leaden in
his hand. Even his crutch, usually so buoyant, now seemed to
simply drag him down, an anchor made of wood.

Two men stood outside the old man's shack. Victor could
see them clearly now. More strangers. They were talking with
the old man.

One was tall and thin, almost emaciated, with a long pointed
chin and curly black hair to the shoulders. He wore a long
black overcoat with an emerald felt collar, and a black silk
top hat.

The other was shorter and fat, and decidedly round—like a
child's first attempt at a circle. He had no neck to speak of.
His nose was puglike and small. His eyes were set deep in his
face, like the seas you could see on the moon. A full moon; it
was so round. He wore a gray coat made of wool.

They seemed the oddest of couples. Two halves of a whole.

As Victor approached, the taller of the strangers reached into his coat and removed a small leather moneybag. Coins jingled as he shook it before him.

The old man snatched it from his hand. He spilled the contents down onto the sand before him, at his feet. He bent down, counted the coins, counted them again, and slipped them deftly back into the bag. Then he looked up, and started as Victor sidled into view.

"Ah, Victor, there you are," he said. He jammed the purse in his coat. "Let me introduce you." He pointed nervously at the tall, emaciated stranger at his side. "This here is Mr. Henry Tipple. This is Victor—the boy I was telling you about." The old man hooked a thumb at the rotund gentleman beside him. "And this here is Biggs. Mr. Oliver Biggs. We met last night at the Cock and Plough."

So that's where the old man had gone, Victor thought. *Yet again.*

"Delighted," Mr. Biggs said, tipping forward in a bow. He was so round that the movement was more of a suggestion than something altogether physical.

Victor hobbled closer. He stared at the two men. Tatters was barking like a rabid wolf to the side. "Be quiet," Victor said. "No, boy. Be still."

The old man whistled and the border collie crawled away, back to the shack.

Victor raised the flounder in his hand. "See what I caught?" he said, beaming. "For Christmas Eve supper. A flounder. Your favorite."

The old man turned the slightest distance to the side. He would not look at Victor's face. "I'm sorry, Victor," he said at last. "But I can't afford to keep you. Times are hard in England now." He stared down at the sand. "These men—Tipple and Biggs. They're undertakers. It may not seem a pleasant business, but it's a decent trade, you'll see. One day you'll come to thank me. I know it in my heart."

Victor felt as though he'd—obviously—completely misunderstood. The words were familiar enough, but they didn't seem to come together. He shook the fish in his hand. "Flounder," he repeated. Like an idiot. Like a fool. It was as if the word, somehow, held mantric qualities, as if it could discourage evil spirits, rewrite the future, recalibrate the basic nature of the universe. The old man took the fish from Victor's hand. Then he turned, without a word, and walked back to the shack. The door closed noiselessly behind him.

"I don't understand," said Victor. He turned and looked at Tipple, then at Biggs. "What does he mean?"

"Are you thick?" said Tipple with a toothless grin. "What do you think he means? You're to come with us."

"With you? Why? Where?"

"Why, to London, boy," squeaked Biggs. "The magic city. The epicenter of civilization. The funnel of the great tornado of the Empire." He smiled. His eyes bulged from his face as if he had been squeezed by some gigantic fist.

"I don't want to go to London. I want to stay here. With Mr. Smith."

"Who's Mr. Smith?"

"Mr. Smith. The old man."

"Oh, that Smith," Tipple said. His voice was deep and sonorous, a striking contrast to his partner's high-pitched squeak.

Biggs fairly giggled. He sputtered and shook. "An apprentice you shall be," he said. "A guildsman, if you will. Don't disappoint your benefactor. A success, lad."

Victor began to back away. There was something about Tipple and Biggs. Perhaps it was their trade. Something still lingered on their clothes. "I'm not going anywhere," he said. "Not with you." Despite the blistering wind which barreled down the beach, the men smelled of death.

He turned to flee, to dash around the corpulent Mr. Biggs, when Tipple snuck up from behind, a piece of driftwood in his hand.

"Welcome aboard," said Tipple, as he brought the wood down on his head. Victor fell. He closed like a flower. Biggs laughed—a shrill, childlike yet soulless sound—and Victor drowned in black seas.

·CHAPTER·
6

DECEMBER, 1830

PETERSFIELD, NEAR THE

WINCHESTER ROAD

VICTOR WOKE INSIDE OF what appeared to be a coffin. He saw the long edge of the box, perceived the putrefying softness of that body beneath him, felt the long emaciated fingers of Mr. Tipple on his face, and screamed. Victor tried to squirm away, but someone else was holding him. Mr. Biggs. He was pressing him down in the coffin, right onto that corpse. He was pressing and holding him down! Then Biggs slipped the lid into place. Blackness reigned. It filled up the casket like oil, drowning him. Victor heard a loud bang and the lid crushed his nose. They were sealing it over him. They were nailing him in! Victor tried with all his might to push the lid off, but it wouldn't budge. He was too late. Another hammer blow, and then another. *Bang, bang.* Victor reached out with his left hand and jammed his fingers through the opening between the coffin and the lid. *Bang, bang.* He felt his fingers being crushed each time they hammered. *Bang, bang.* Then they gave up.

Victor held his breath. Now that the lid was almost closed, the air was filled with the most nauseating stench. It was the man below him, the corpse on which he lay. Victor had crushed the rotting body with the weight of his own form. He gagged. He turned to vomit. But there was nowhere to go. His left hand was still wedged between the coffin and the lid. His fingers pulsed with pain but he dared not scream, or groan, or even whisper. He could hear Biggs and Tipple outside. He turned his head. Slowly. He swiveled his neck with great care. He peered through the crack pried apart by his fingers. Mr. Tipple was standing a few feet away. He was lit by a lamp, and his frame was so narrow and twisted, so perplexingly crooked, that at first Victor took him for shadow. He was standing in what appeared to be a graveyard. Victor could see several headstones through the crack. Then Biggs swung around into view. He was carrying a shovel. It was wooden. He joined Mr. Tipple.

"I hear Plum sold a thing for ten guineas," said Biggs.

"Izzied from some church 'all, no doubt." Mr. Tipple took another wooden shovel and gently worked the dirt away from a headstone. Then he jammed it down into the earth. Biggs dug beside him. They heaved and worked the soil together. It was half-frozen and obdurate. They cursed as they dug. The ground was intractable.

"Why not jus' kill 'em and be done with it?" said Tipple. "No diggin' then."

"No broken backs," added Biggs. "Crack her open, I say. Fish 'er out."

"You 'eard the good doctor. Coffin, too, Mr. Biggs. We

'ave to look proper. A pair of undertakers is what we are. Fancy trouncing down Piccadilly with a thing flappin' about in the wagon. That would be a sight now, wouldn't it? Like a flag. Like a pennant, Mr. Biggs. Our colors."

There was a dull thud. Biggs had found bottom. He tapped at the earth. "Got her, Mr. Tipple."

The thin man dropped a grappling hook tied to a rope into the ground. He held the rope out with care. He concentrated. The length of his arm—stretched out in that manner, with that rope hanging down from his fingers—made him look like a fisherman holding a pole. He moved his hand slightly and then snapped on the rope with a solid quick flick of the wrist.

"We'll be sucking pork fat from our fingers by mornin'. And I don't mean long pig, to be sure, Mr. Biggs. Though they say that it's fair with some finger-and-thumb." Tipple hauled on the rope. Biggs jumped in beside him. They pulled and they yanked and the crown of a casket shot up from the earth.

"Thar she blows," uttered Biggs. He squealed and wrapped himself round the coffin. He heaved. The casket slithered out of the dirt. Tipple helped him drag it over to the wagon.

"A job well done," he said. "Happy Christmas to you, Mr. Biggs."

"And to you, too, Mr. Tipple."

They lifted the muddy coffin. They carried it aloft, and over, and laid it down directly on top of Victor's casket. Victor yanked his hand back from the crack just as the lid pressed down. He felt the wood against his face. He felt the top slide into place. A deathly silence filled the coffin. It was pitch-black. The crack was sealed. He was trapped now. The air filled quickly with the smell of rotting flesh mixed with the scent of his own vomit. He clenched his teeth. He closed his eyes. The wagon shook. He felt it pitch and heave. They were traveling, and this notion filled him with a pale relief. Perhaps Tipple and Biggs hadn't lied. Perhaps they were going to London, after all. To the magic city. The epicenter of civilization. Into the funnel of the great tornado of the Empire.

PART II

·CHAPTER·
7

VICTOR TRIED TO FORGET the journey," Dr. Lambro said.

Colonel Maxwell had removed his jacket and now stood almost at attention at the doctor's side. Lambro was prepping for the operation.

The boy had been laid out lengthwise across the kitchen table. He was naked from the waist up; his blood-encrusted shirt had been removed. The body seemed to glow within the lambent lamplight. The doctor had scrubbed the skin. The broken ribs looked like two icebergs adrift on an Arctic sea.

"Years later," Dr. Lambro said, "Victor still dreamed about that smell, the pressing blackness, and the constant shaking of the coffin as they staggered up the road to London. He thought that it would never end."

The doctor selected his sharpest scalpel. He pressed the tip into the skin. He felt the blade go in. Then he ran it gently down the young boy's chest, peeling away the epidermis.

"Blot up that blood," he said. Colonel Maxwell leaned over and padded the area with a clean cloth. The doctor sliced again.

"Victor has the life of the soldier."

"How's that?"

"Long periods of boredom and maddening inactivity, followed by seconds of pure hell. What happened next? Don't keep me in suspense, man. Out with the tale."

For a night and a day they kept moving, they kept bouncing along, Lambro said. And Biggs never seemed to stop talking. At first it was comforting. The sound kept his terrors at bay. But after hours and hours of irrelevant discourse, of constant complaining and puffy bravado, Victor grew tired of listening. In truth, despite the most gruesome aroma, he preferred the mute company of the corpse at his back. . . .

Famished and parched, bruised from the journey, Victor grew more and more anxious. On the second day, the noises that seeped through the coffin grew fuller, more varied. They were entering the capital city. Strange smells competed with the odor of death, despite the various pieces of cloth that Victor had torn from his shirt and stuffed up his nostrils. He could hear horses and the dull mooing of cows. He could hear carriages clip-clopping along, and men's voices, and the grind of machinery, and the chatter of women and children.

Finally, on what he guessed was the evening of the second day, the carriage came to a full stop. Victor waited several minutes, thinking it was yet another false alarm. Then he heard the coffin above him slide free, pulled away. He felt his own casket heaved upward, and over, to the side, borne aloft. They carried him onward and upward, then down a long corridor. Somehow, he sensed they were traveling indoors. The timbre of the echoes had changed, and he could feel the casket banging on what he could only guess were stone walls. They bore him along and aloft, up some stairs, down some corridor. They ascended and finally stopped.

Victor could hear himself breathing. It was as if he had carried the casket himself, on his own; he felt out of breath. Then a thump, and a grind. They were prying the lid off. A cool breath of air kissed his face. Light shot through the crack. Victor stirred. He could move his head slightly. *Bang, bang,* and the lid lifted off. He was free. He sat up in the coffin. He felt giddy and light. Tipple and Biggs stood beside him. Victor took in the room. It was dark. Tipple was holding a candle, but its glow was anemic. Then Victor realized he was still shallow breathing. He took a great breath. He breathed out. Then he turned.

Pale eyes stared back. There were dozens and dozens of them. Animals! Some were free, some in cages. There were owls, hawks, and ferrets, and fancy white mice. There were monkeys and parrots and peacocks and snakes. And beside them were children. Mostly standing about. Of all ages. Boys and girls, tall and short, blond and dark—but invariably thin. They stood there and stared. And Victor stared back.

"Out you go, then," said Tipple. He prodded the boy in the ribs.

Victor climbed out of the coffin. Biggs passed him a mug of cold water. Victor swallowed it down in three gulps. Biggs gave him his crutch. "Welcome to the menagerie," he said, beaming. "Where we're all simply one of the animals." He snickered and bobbed. He picked up the lid of the casket and dropped it in place. "Shall we go, Mr. Tipple?"

"After you, Mr. Biggs." Tipple set the candle on the coffin. They picked up the casket, one at each end, and staggered away toward the door.

Victor watched it slam shut with a bang. He heard the scrape of a bolt, then the echo of footsteps retreating. Somewhere, an owl hooted. He turned. Someone lit up a Lucifer. The match sputtered and burned. They were in some kind of attic room, a storage space. Huge beams supported the roof above, cathedral-style. The crossbeams were covered with birds. Other creatures, too. There were lizards and possums and rats. . . .

"What do we have here?" a boy said, drawing near. He was tall and well built, with blond hair and blue eyes. He was carrying a candle. "Blow my eyes if it ain't another blackamoor, Master Spendlove," he continued. He laughed and Victor thought he looked grotesquely handsome. Despite his good looks, his face was marred by a harelip, a congenital oddity that Victor had seen before in Modena.

"Right you are, Pike," said another.

The boy called Pike stopped advancing. He turned his attention for a moment toward a small dark boy at his feet. "A playmate for Nico, perhaps," he continued. "Two peas in a pod."

"Black-eyed peas," Spendlove said. He was pockmarked and gawky. His skin clung to his cheekbones, as if there were simply too much of his face. He took a step closer to Pike.

Pike lifted his foot and pressed it to the neck of the youngster called Nico beside him. Then he kicked him away.

"Stop that," said Victor.

"What's that? He speaks English. Damn my eyes, Master Spendlove, he does. A priest's bastard, I'll wager." Nico squirmed to the side but Pike kicked him again.

"Leave him be," Victor said, moving closer.

"Or what?" Pike replied. "What will you do? Bite your tongue, knowing kovy, if you know what's proper. Or I'll put a spoke in your weal."

A girl with long dark hair and chestnut brown eyes swept into view from the shadows. She wore a pretty blue dress and her hair was done up with blue ribbons. "Why don't you leave him alone, Master Stringall? What's the boy done to you?" Her accent was strange.

"Reinforcements," said Spendlove. He laughed with derision. "Oh, no," he continued. "What to do?" He pantomimed terror. "A spud eater approaches. A Papist. Quick, run for your lives!"

"Disheartening, it is," added Pike. "A girl and a cripple."
Victor hobbled still closer.

"Give him a topper," said Spendlove. "He's askin' for it."
Pike smiled. He crouched down and waited for Victor. He kicked Nico again.

"I'm warning you," Victor said. "Leave him be."
For the first time, the boy on the floor looked at Victor. He was smiling. He was dark and quite tiny, with large soulful eyes, chocolate brown. He wore a floppy wool hat of indeterminate color, a tattered gray shirt, and a jacket, shiny with

grease. He smiled and kept smiling, and looked up at Pike. He just couldn't stop grinning and Victor surmised, in that instant, in a flash, understood: There was something terribly wrong with the boy.

"It's not so important," Nico said in Italian, with a thick Tuscan accent.

Victor found himself smiling at the sound of the words. Then he stopped, shook his head. "It's important to me," he replied in Italian. "Stand up and defend yourself, countryman. And I'll fight by your side."

Pike walked up and slapped Victor. "We speak the King's English in London," he said matter-of-factly.

Victor did not even hesitate. The crutch flew, arced about. He swept the boy's legs out from directly beneath him. Pike struck the floor hard. The candle fell to the planking but it did not go out. Pike cursed and jumped back to his feet.

"You bloody bur-head," he cried, circling. "I'll spill your insides for that!" A blade danced in his hands. "Blow my eyes if there shan't be another tucked up for you." Nico picked up the candle. "You think you've done the trick up, do you? You think you've . . ."

He hadn't even finished his sentence when the crutch whirled again. Pike tried to duck. He tried to step back but he tripped on some animal, a tortoise or turtle. The crutch struck his left cheek with a sickening *thwack*. He flew through the darkness, out of sight. He fell on his back. There was a loud bang as he bounced off the wall. Beasts scurried away. Fowl flew and snakes slithered. Pike cursed and ran back. He was furious now. His pale skin had turned red. Blood ran down his cheek.

Victor prepared himself. He glanced at the girl, but she didn't even seem to be watching. She was looking away. "That's enough," Victor said.

This last phrase only seemed to spur the boy on. Pike charged. He flung out his arms, tried to grab Victor's neck, but Victor simply side-stepped away. He brought his crutch down and around. It struck Pike on the back, sending him sprawling again through the darkness. There was a loud bang as he struck the wall, and then another crash as paneling gave way. This time Pike didn't return to the light. He stayed in the shadows. Victor could hear him crawling about in the dark. Spendlove waded in after him, intercepting his friend, and together they slithered away.

Victor hobbled over to Nico. He lifted the boy to his feet.

"Are you a Knight of Malta?" the boy asked in Italian.

Victor laughed. "Heavens, no."

"You fight like one."

Victor straightened the boy's greasy jacket. His hat had fallen off in the struggle. Victor looked about the floor, but it was gone. He reached into his pants and pulled out his own tricolor hat. He flattened the edges, pressed the creases with care. Then he handed the hat to the boy.

Nico stared down upon it as if it were the most wonderful thing in the world. He marveled at the workmanship, the stitching, the troika of colors. He glanced up with a grin. "For me?"

"For you. From Modena. Up the Carbonari," he said, raising his fist.

Nico smiled. He put the hat on his head. It suited him.

Despite his constant smiling, the boy's dark mournful eyes imbued his aspect with a doleful countenance. But the hat added whimsy, some comic relief. It was a counterpoint to his natural melancholia, a beacon of frivolity against petulant skies. Like his smile. *"Mille grazie,"* said Nico as he paraded about. "How do I look?"

Victor winked his left eye, pursed his lips, and nodded with gravity in a gesture that was purely Italian. Nico swelled.

Just then, the girl in the blue dress approached. She seemed to have no problem traversing the floor, despite all the children and animals. It was difficult to see in the room. The candle that Nico was carrying was feeble. Then she stopped and looked off to the side. "That was kind of you," she began. "My name is Rebecca. And this," she said, pointing, "is Nico. Hereafter, your lifelong companion." She laughed. It was a light and airy laugh, untethered by gravity. It seemed to fly through the darkness. She had an odd accent.

"My name is Victor," he added. "From Modena, Emilia-Romagna. Near Bologna."

"Nico's from Florence, in Tuscany."

"So I gathered. And you," he continued, feeling suddenly tongue-tied. "You're from . . ."

". . . Carrick-on-Shannon. In Ireland. But I'm a London girl now."

"Where exactly are we?"

"The rookery of St. Giles. Master Hartley's house. You'll find out. These are his animals," she added, pointing.

"What are they for?"

"We rent them," said Nico. He dropped to his knees. He

picked up a rabbit and stroked it. It lay in his arms like a pet. "From the Master."

"Who's the Master?"

"*Padroni,*" Nico said in Italian. "*Proveditori.*"

"*Proveditori?*"

"*Io viaggio al mondo con a commedia,*" Nico said.

Victor was taken aback. Literally, the phrase meant he was wandering the world with a theater troupe. But the truth was far darker. Back in Modena, Victor had heard of *Padroni,* or "Masters," buying young boys from impoverished parents with promises of teaching them tricks or theatrical skills. In truth, each was sold into slavery, bonded servitude, to be trained as a beggar's apprentice. None ever returned.

"It's four pennies a day for the use of the attic," Nico said. "Two shillings for wax Siamese twins; three and sixpence for an organ with figures that waltz; two shillings for porcupines, or four with an organ; three shillings for a monkey in uniform; one and sixpence for a box with white mice; two shillings a tortoise; and three for a monkey what rides a dog's back."

"What for?" Victor asked. He was amazed at Nico's memory for numbers.

"Why, to beg!" said Rebecca. "It makes us more plaintive. You won't get a farthing with naught but your face, no matter how pitiful. There are simply too many of us. You need something different, something funny or silly or odd. And then, once you have them, once they're crowded about you, you can cough up your craw, tell your story. Pinch more pennies that way."

"You mean you're all beggars."

"The best of us," said Rebecca. "Some will take more than

charity when the crowd is the thickest. But the Master discourages thieving. Calls it 'yesterday's supper.' Because that's all that you'll have once he pushes you out. Thievin's quick tuck, if you please; a meal that you have on the hurry. It won't feed you through winter. Unless you cozy the Dicity, to get out of the snow. It's been a hard winter, has it not, Master Victor?"

It was the first time she had used his name. Victor stared at her. She did not seem to want to look directly at him. She peered into the darkness. Then she added, "Wait, what's that?" She cocked her head.

Victor stared at the shadows. He could hear children whispering. He could hear animals crawling about. "What's what?" he said, but she put a hand to his lips. Her fingers felt cool and surprisingly soft. They were tiny. *Like the fingers of a child,* he thought, though she must have been twelve or thirteen.

"Shhhh," said Rebecca. Then she suddenly vanished. She seemed to dissolve between curtains of blackness.

Victor had a hard time keeping up. The girl darted between the sleeping children, around the animals and birds, as if she could see in the dark. After a moment, she slowed down and cocked her head again. She knelt on the floor by the wall. This is where Pike had smashed against the paneling. Victor could just make out a piece of planking on the floor. He knelt down beside her. "What is it?" he said.

"Be quiet!" she whispered.

Victor squirmed. He looked into the hole.

"What do you see?" she asked with impatience.

Victor peered through the opening. He could just make out a pair of figures below. One was facing the hole. He was wearing a cutaway. He was stooped and quite thin, with a few strands of gray hair atop the wide dome of his head. The surface was sprinkled with moles, beauty marks. They seemed to be all over his scalp, on his neck and his face. He was talking to another man with his back to the opening. "I see two men."

"Describe them to me."

"Take a look for yourself if you—"

"Describe them!"

Victor sighed. "One has dark spots all over his face. The other is facing away. No, wait."

The man turned for a moment. He was wearing a top hat and black linen tailcoat. He was holding a cane. There was something . . . Victor strained and peered closer. The head of the cane. It was carved out of ivory. And it looked like an elephant's head.

"And the cargo from Portsmouth?" the stranger began.

"Safe and sound, sir. On the road to your house."

"Was it fresh?"

"Why, of course, sir," the man with the moles answered smugly. "Just come off a schooner from Russia and Hamburg, via Sunderland, just as you asked. All the symptoms, good doctor: dehydration, diarrhea, and vomiting. All the symptoms, as ordered."

"Very good. Did you square the account with Tipple and Biggs?"

"I did, sir. But I won't trouble you now with details. A man of your eminence has more pressing affairs, I don't wonder. All in good time." He started rubbing his hands. "All in good time." He smiled and nodded and bobbed.

Victor felt Rebecca hover beside him. He could feel the heat from her cheek. He could smell the scent of her hair. She pressed her mouth to his ear. "What does he look like?" she whispered. "The other man?"

"I can't see," he replied. "He's faced the wrong way."

"Look again," she insisted.

Victor pressed his eye to the hole. "He's still looking away. I can't see him. He's wearing a top hat and tailcoat."

She drew him still closer. He could feel her warm breath in his ear. "Is he holding a cane?"

"A cane? Yes, made of ivory, I think. Shaped like an elephant's head."

Rebecca withdrew. Victor turned from the wall. He could just see her face in the candlelight. It looked to be carved out of stone. "Do you know him?" he said.

The girl didn't respond. She was looking away. She kept staring off into space.

"The man with the cane. Rebecca? Rebecca, who is he?"

"Master's master," she said, turning toward him. She was staring right into his face. She was looking right at him, and yet it was obvious—for the first time, it dawned on him—the girl with the chestnut brown eyes couldn't see.

·CHAPTER· 8

VICTOR WAS OVERWHELMED by the city. Compared to Modena, London was vast, a universe unto itself, stretching nine miles from Fulham to Poplar, and seven from Highbury to Camberwell, not counting the city's great suburbs such as Lambeth and Paddington. It was twice the size of Paris, and six times the size of Rome.

Redesigned after the Great Fire, the streets were narrow and winding, somehow accommodating the almost two million souls who called London home. There were hundreds of little factories and workshops, mostly in the city and inner suburbs, making everything from clothing in Stepney to clockworks in Clerkenwell. Along the river flourished trades linked with shipping: sugar-refining, rubber, and soap; chemicals, paint, and tobacco. Southwark was the center of flour-milling, tanning, and brewing; Rotherhithe host to the building of ships. Another hundred thousand people found employment in government, education, and medicine; in banking, insurance, and the law. And the city was growing . . . at a rate of a quarter million each decade.

Victor learned all this from Nico, who seemed to have an encyclopedic memory for figures, although he could not tie his own shoes. The boy had been in London for two years, brought there originally by a *Padrone* named Ricci; but the Pisan had perished of dysentery, and the boy had been passed on to Hartley.

"If you walked every day, for the rest of your life," Nico told him, "you would never see it all—for new bits are being added each day."

Because they were fellow countrymen, the Master fixed Nico to Victor, and the young boy took pride in his work as a guide. He showed Victor his London. They would rise before dawn, when it was still oppressively dark, still freezing and damp, and make their way through the streets. Since the omnibus was slow and expensive, and the narrow lanes generally clogged, they would walk. The streets were already packed with local workers heading off to nearby building sites and docks to find day work. Roads not cobblestoned were easily shattered by traffic. Fine ladies lifted their skirts to cross over, handing a coin now and then to boys known as sweepers, who brushed away only some of the dust and the dung. It was a foolhardy exercise. The carts, cabs, and omnibuses that challenged the streets sent up showers of water, and horse dung and mud, which only seemed to add to the cinder-black canopy smothering the city. Every now and again, Victor noticed, came a "London particular," a fog brought about by low cloud, tepid air, and brown billowing masses of sulphurous smoke.

Not even the glaring gaslights of the gin palaces, nor the hundreds of miles of new streetlamps, could penetrate the gloom brought about by the three million tons of coal burned each year in the city.

Victor's favorite section of London was the river. Only a handful of vessels could tie up on the north bank of the Thames. The rest lay at anchor, in the heart of the flow, side to side. They were forced to unload onto barges. From there, all the imports were brought to the Custom House. According to Nico, the building collected more than half of the taxes paid each year to the realm, around £30 million, compared to the £10 million earned from levies on income and property. Victor could see why. More than one hundred ships came and went from the docks every day, not counting the steam tugs that dragged the great ships into place, nor the passenger steamers. Victor loved to watch the sailing ships and their lighters, the sloops and the barges negotiate the river amid a deluge of shouting and cursing. Coal-whippers and stevedores sweated and sang as they unloaded the colliers which brought mountains of coal from north England to London each day. A tangle of rigging seemed to girdle the sky. Ships were anchored two or three abreast, in two tiers, as far as the eye could see, and steamboats and barges and wherries wiggled between them. They were carrying sugar and rum, tobacco and cocoa and coffee from the Americas. They bore palm oil and ivory from Africa. And in turn, they were loaded with cases of Birmingham metalware, and with goods made of cotton from Manchester.

Victor's least favorite section was Smithfield. When he wasn't being versed in the ways of the beggar, he would accompany

Nico there to fetch feed for the animals that Master Hartley rented out to the children. The center of the largest meat market in the city, one required a strong stomach and fleet feet to negotiate Smithfield. Animal and human excrement, urine, fat, and blood mixed together to form a permanent pool of nauseating filth five inches deep along every street. While local bylaws forbade the emission of blood from area slaughterhouses, it was a fixture of each walkway anyway. Much of the slaughter was conducted underground, in basements and subterranean abattoirs, and passersby were frequently subjected to hot blasts of blood-splattered air, the last breaths of beasts as they fell to the ax. Many sheep were skinned while alive. And horses were frequently stabled in the putrefying remains of their fellows, maimed and starving, awaiting their own executions. Somehow they knew. Victor could see it in their pitiful eyes. The scene was made even more horrible by the beatings. In the marketplace, the cattle were kept in "drove circles," consisting of fifteen beasts or so with their heads jammed together and their rumps out, exposed to the gouging of goads. And it wasn't just the slaughterhouses that poisoned the neighborhood. It was the sausagemakers and tanners, the cat- and rabbit-fur dressers, the bladder blowers and bone dealers, the cat-gut manufacturers. Very little was wasted. The meanest morsel, Victor realized, had value.

Animals came to Smithfield from all over Great Britain. Drovers walked fifteen to twenty miles each day, sleeping out in the fields with their cargo to prevent theft from rustlers. An ox lost twenty pounds in weight, Nico said, for every hundred miles of the journey. The three weeks it took to walk from the

Highlands in Scotland affected the meat, unless the animal had time to recover, pasturing in the grazing counties of Leicestershire, Lincolnshire, and Norfolk. The last stop was Islington before the charge down St. John Street to Smithfield.

Monday was the busiest morning in Smithfield—the main beef-trading day, with two thousand cattle and fifteen thousand sheep changing hands. Streets to the east of the area, as distant as Barbican, were solid with animal traffic. The migration form Islington—where London drovers took on the herds—started at eleven o'clock, Sabbath eve, and lasted until five in the morning. Since the animals were forced to share the road with urban traffic, accidents invariably occurred. It was not uncommon for a bullock to break loose from the herd in a panic, and to run helter-skelter through the streets. Indeed, it wasn't always an accident.

One time, when Nico and Victor were buying feed for the Master, they watched Pike poke a stick up a bullock's behind. The terrified animal took off down the street, bellowing and kicking, shattering windows, sending pedestrians flying. Pike and Spendlove took advantage of the chaos. As the crowd dashed about, they picked dozens of pockets, and pinched food from the carts of street vendors.

But that was quick tuck, as Rebecca had called it. Master Hartley looked down upon stealing. Most of the time, they earned money the "right way," as the Master defined it—by begging.

The majority of the children who made their living in this manner had been forced into the streets by their parents. Don't come home, they were told, until you've scrounged up your supper . . . by begging or stealing or worse. Few came home empty-handed. Those who didn't succeed hardly ever returned. They became part of the great sea of children that washed through the streets of the city. You could see them each morning asleep under stalls at the various markets, in the shrubs of Hyde Park, stacked in piles in the haystacks of Marylebone, in the warm kilns of East Ender brickyards, or curled in the barrels of coopers in Whitechapel.

A variety of philanthropic societies debated the cause of this homelessness. It was the vast number of abandoned wives, they surmised; tens of thousands of men had been wounded or killed in the wars with Napoleon.

Others believed it was the outcome of the population explosion. Some thirty thousand babies were born in the city each year. It was no wonder, they said, that the city was bulging at the seams with the homeless.

More than fifteen thousand boys roamed the streets of the city each day, only gaining their beer and their bread by begging and lying and cheating, by sweeping the footwear of ladies, holding gentlemen's horses, barely clothed and half-fed, homeless, friendless, and generally unloved. They were alternately the inmates of ramshackle workhouses, of prisons and treadmills, sliding down through gradations of misery, on their way to the hulk or the gibbet or grave.

The Vagrancy Act labeled each person who was picked up for begging an "idle and disorderly person." And the London Society for the Suppression of Mendicity employed a number of plainclothes enforcers who plied through the streets and arrested those suspected of vagrancy. One way to skirt Dicity, as the officers were called, was by doing far more than just idling for alms with a cup and pathetic expression. A new generation of vagrants was emerging, combining the role of the outcast and street entertainer, catering to that hunger for spectacle that drove Londoners to the shoddiest penny gaff theater. Most Londoners were illiterate: One third of men, and almost one half of women, couldn't even sign their own names in the register on the day of their weddings. Cut off from the world of books and of weeklies, of newspapers, even, they gathered instead at rough caravan shows featuring midgets and strange foreign animals, waxworks and people with the oddest deformities. Those like Victor, who could barely afford food, found a modest entertainment by simply gawking at pineapples, oranges, and other strange fruit at Covent Garden. But he had little time for such play.

Victor had to scrounge up four pennies a day for his lodging, and his food cost at least one and sixpence. Since Victor worked with Nico in caring for the animals, the Master allowed him use of the beasts without charge—those not previously taken by paying customers, that is. And Victor used them. As Rebecca had warned him, his face was not enough to filch farthings from the jaded fingers of Londoners. At first he tried juggling, but his shattered leg and crutch got in the way. Next, he carried a board on his head, like some gigantic hat, crowned with the busts of famous poets and philosophers. It was but a mild success. Then he tried mice and guinea pigs, marmots and porcupines, tortoises and snakes. Each drew its own special crowd. His natural melancholy air proved helpful. Like Nico, Victor had that plaintive Italian look about him that Londoners found both pitiful and exotic, oddly endearing. And then, of course, there was his injury.

The people were used to the tricks of the poor: the Lurkers, who carried false documents showing deprivation by wreck, fire, or accident; Cadgers on the Downright, who begged from door to door; Cadgers on the Fly, like Victor, who begged from passersby; Shallow Lays, who wandered aimlessly in rags on frigid days; and Screevers, who chalked appeals upon pavements. But unlike so many charlatans, Victor was obviously genuine. There was no faking that leg.

Victor tried everything, but it wasn't until he struck upon the Happy Family that he finally started to prosper. A Happy Family was made by joining warring species in a single cage—like cats and birds, or mice and cats, ferrets and rats. The juxtaposition of such animals often startled the most world-weary pedestrian, made him tarry, then stop, made him stare for a moment, long enough to provide Victor with some sort of opening. Uttering a few words in his accent was usually sufficient. The flat, as such dupes were labeled, would look upon Victor—his clear hazel eyes, black locks, trembling lips—and nine times out of ten plunge his hand in his pockets. On a good day, especially if Victor were lucky enough to draw the dancing monkeys—by far the most expensive and most lucrative display—he could earn more than a guinea, or twenty-one shillings, in one place.

Of course, one begged at one's peril. Many children were victimized by thieves, brothel-keepers, procurers of pickpockets and press-gangs. One always had to keep a sharp lookout, warned Rebecca. The formal police were far less troublesome than the Dicity. The Peelers, or Metropolitan Police, instituted by Sir Robert Peel the previous year, were so unfamiliar that they were still known by most Londoners as the "New Police," and by the children as Bluebottles, because of their uniforms.

Everything was changing. The New Police were but one symbol of the evolution. It was as if—in this new age of gaslighting and the telegraph—the city could no longer afford to expose its dark underbelly. England had a new king. Railway lines were being lain down at a frightening pace. New scientific discoveries were being made every day. Vast tracts of hovels were being razed for new middle-class housing. The pending Reform Bill would soon expand suffrage. Society was evolving. There was a sense that beggars like Victor, the street folk, the homeless, would soon be a thing of the past.

It was only later that Victor fully understood all these things. Back then, in the midst of this sea of change, the things which preoccupied him were far simpler, more immediate: his next meal; avoiding Pike and Spendlove; and where would he be sleeping that night. The sound of the old world crashing down all around him was drowned out by the wailing of the new age being born.

On this particular evening, three weeks after his arrival in the city, after a long day of begging, Victor returned home to St. Giles, pondering his new life, and all the wondrous and horrific things in it. He wandered down the narrow streets and alleys of the rookery, hopping from one rotting pile of vegetables to the next, trying to avoid the rancid pools of urine and the fly-specked piles of human feces that oozed up from sewers and the doorless privies of the street. Most people simply threw their excrement and trash into the gutter. But, despite the endless gloomy days of fog and drizzle, there never seemed to be enough rain to wash it all away.

Victor scrambled down Jacob's Alley—twenty feet long but only two feet wide. He climbed across two broken lots, swung south down Thompson, up Mudlark Lane, and home.

The house was one of thirty-six that stood around a court-yard. It was a three-room, two-story building, a Tudor, with a crumbling façade, and a little garden in back, filled with trash and wooden crates that the children sometimes broke apart and burned upstairs when coal grew scarce. The Master usually waited for them at the door. He liked to check the children's earnings, have them pay their debts off, before letting them in. He stood there with his hands out, bobbing his head, cooing at them. His mostly bald, mole-covered dome gleamed in the candlelight as he checked their pockets one by one.

On days when flats were plentiful, and he had the time, Victor might indulge in some supper—a penn'orth, or penny's worth of eels, usually stewed. But today had been particularly anemic. It had rained heavily and few had bothered to take a momentary peek into his cage, and even fewer had tarried long enough to pluck a farthing from their pockets. Most days he could only afford a penny loaf and a penny's worth of milk for breakfast, another penny loaf and a morsel of cheese for dinner at noon, and a pint of coffee with a slice of quartern loaf for "tea."

He made his way upstairs, to the attic. Two dozen people lived in the house, most of them children. Nico had already returned. He was feeding the animals. Victor helped him. The darker it grew, the more crowded the attic, as children returned from their begging.

Nico had a strange way with the beasts. It was almost as if he were one of them. Sometimes he'd urge Victor to get down on the floor, on his hands and his knees, and observe the world like an animal. He'd take Victor's hand, and gently run his fingers across the back of some monkey or mouse, down the leg of some kitten, caressing their tendons and bones. He said it would help him ken beasts. It appeared, on occasion, as if Nico actually spoke with the animals, really knew what they felt, or were thinking.

But this night Victor didn't want to play games, or to talk, or to be around anyone. He was tired of the pressing crowds, the chatter of bottomless mouths. He wanted to simply get away. So he climbed the ladder at the back of the attic and lifted the hatch in the roof. He climbed out, and then up, and around the thin parapet to his favorite spot. He looked out on the neighborhood at the courtyard below, the crumbling houses around him, at the vast, dizzying lightscape of London.

A dense canopy of smoke hovered over the roofs and towers of the city like fog. It was impossible to tell where London started or ended, for the buildings stretched not only to the horizon on each side, but far into the distance. With the advancing shades of twilight and the dense fumes from the chimneys, the city seemed to bleed into the sky, so that there was no way of distinguishing heaven from earth.

Victor sat there and thought about Modena, about his parents, about the light and sound and smells of the city he had loved, trying to push away the malodorous monstrosity that glistened about him, pulsing with life, with the blood-engorged hearts of millions of strangers. He had been saved from the sea only to be thrown up onto this island of filth and disease and despair. *Why?* he thought. Why had God bothered? To what end? And he pondered yet another odd fact that his friend Nico had snagged on the way: The slave trade had been abolished in 1807. And yet one could still own a slave. One could still be a slave.

"Victor!" It was Rebecca. Her head was poking through the opening in the roof. "Victor, come down. The Master is calling," she cried.

Victor climbed down from the parapet, crossed over the roof, and slipped down the ladder. "What does he want at this hour?" he inquired.

"You must drive me," she said.

"Where to?"

Rebecca kept walking. She didn't even slow down. When she reached the attic door, she pulled it open, turned, and trained her sightless eyes upon him. "To hell and back," she said.

·CHAPTER· 9

AT REBECCA'S INSISTENCE, Victor took the long way around into Mayfair, a most affluent section of London's West End. He drove the Master's carriage, a rather run-down calèche, with ludicrous springs. It was raining again. It beat down upon him in great solid sheets while Rebecca reclined in the cab. But he didn't mind. He was happy to drive her. Of all of Hartley's cadgers—with the exception of Nico—he felt most at ease with Rebecca. But each time he tried to make conversation, to say something of interest, she barely responded. She seemed sullen and worried this evening, distracted by more pressing affairs. Whatever they were, she wouldn't share them with Victor. And this made him sad, to his utmost surprise. He had never felt this way before, about anyone. He didn't know what to do with these feelings.

When they arrived at the address which Rebecca had told him, Victor pulled out an umbrella from under the seat and escorted his charge to the door. The house was a massive affair, made of brick, with twin gables, mostly covered in ivy. Two large windows faced the street, aglow with gas lighting, revealing a foyer of sorts and a library. The walls of the second room were crowded with books, row upon row, of every conceivable color and shape. It seemed splendidly opulent, warm, and cozy inside. A fence ran around the perimeter of the property. A dog stood outside in the rain. They rang the bell and a butler appeared almost instantly.

He was tall with a tiny bald head and weak chin. He was wearing a cinder-black cutaway. Victor looked past him. The floor of the hallway was covered with marble, creamy Arabescato, from Carrara, near Genoa. Oil paintings of seascapes dotted the walls, which were paneled with walnut, and a great wooden staircase curled around at the back.

The butler looked down, frowned and pouted, and motioned the girl to come forward. Then he held out his hand, stopping Victor from entering. "You're to wait," he said sternly. "In the street." Before Victor could say anything, the door slammed in his face. He looked up. Despite the mist and the rain, he could make out a figure in a window above him. Someone stood there, half hidden by curtains, looking out. But his face was concealed by the steam on the glass.

Victor went back to the carriage. He climbed up in the back. He sat there and waited and waited and waited. He watched as the rain came and went, came again. He studied the figures that dashed through the streets. There were couples with black cloth umbrellas. There were sailors and Bluebottles. There were men with long coats and fur collars. Some stared as he sat there and waited and watched. Then they drifted away.

The mansion squatted on the far side of the fence. The two windows that faced the street began to take on the aspect of rectangular eyes in a giant square face, bearded with ivy. The front door was the nose. And the walkway that glimmered with rain in the gaslight looked just like a tongue, rolling out to the street. Victor thought he would go mad from the waiting. One hour passed, and then two, and then three. Carriage upon carriage sped by. Horses whinnied. Drunkards laughed. Somewhere a piano was ringing. He could hear the same song, playing over and over, in sync with the patter of the rain on the canopy. Over and over. The same endless notes.

Victor tried to sleep, but the carriage was windy and cold. He huddled up in a horse rug. He reclined on the seat. But try as he might, he couldn't get Rebecca's face out of his head. Each time he closed his eyes, he saw her before him, her chestnut brown hair with blue ribbons, her delicate eyebrows, her lips and that dimple which appeared every time that she smiled, but just on one side. He sat up. He shook his head. "To blazes with it," he said. He scrambled down from the carriage and made his way across the pavement to the fence. There. He had noticed it before. Beside that giant rhododendron bush. One of the railings in the iron fence was bent a little, or loose, or . . . He hobbled over. He prodded the railing with his crutch. Yes, it was loose. He looked down the street. No one was coming. He pushed the railing aside. He jammed his body in the opening. It was a tight fit. He held his breath, he heaved, and was through. After a moment, he hauled his crutch in after him. Then he turned and saw the dog.

It was an Irish wolfhound, and it was huge, three feet tall

at the withers. The great dog was growling, head slunk, lips curled, exposing giant teeth. They seemed to glimmer in the gaslight streaming from the windows. Victor held his hand out. He said a few low words. He leaned a little closer and the dog came up to him and sniffed his fingers and wrapped himself around his shattered leg. The dog was cold. Victor petted his wiry gray fur. He held him close, whispering words of tenderness in Italian. The dog seemed to understand. He sat down, half on Victor's feet. He nuzzled against him.

Victor looked up at the house as he patted the dog. It seemed to stretch back for a good hundred yards or more. It was massive, a true mansion, bigger than any he'd seen in Modena, except for the Duke of Este's estate. Window upon window ran back through the shrubbery, glowing with gaslight. It was three stories high.

He made his way deeper into the garden. The sound of the music seemed to grow louder and louder the farther he walked. That interminable tune. Like a hand organ in the paws of a monkey. Over and over. He pushed his way through tangles of shrubbery, between branches of laurels and great rhododendrons. The music. It was coming from that window. Just up ahead. He scrambled still closer.

The bushes gave way to a path made of gravel. He hobbled across. It wasn't a window at all. It was a set of French doors. He tarried beside them. He paused for a moment, trying to settle his heart. Then he peeked around the corner and stared.

Victor couldn't believe his eyes. He cleared the rain from the window with the sleeve of his coat. He saw horses and rabbits and piglets and unicorns, decked in ribbons and jewels, in ornately carved saddles of gold-painted wood. They were monstrous and spinning about. It was some kind of machine. Victor pressed his face closer. A merry-go-round! He had seen them before in Modena. But at carnivals, and not inside houses. The walls of the cream-colored room were alternately covered with mirrors and screens, brightly painted with pastoral scenes. It was like a child's dream. There were toys and stuffed animals everywhere, of every description: life-size puppets and soldiers in beaver fur hats; drums and musical instruments; and great balls of rope, three feet high. Victor froze, caught his breath. He steadied himself on his crutch. On the merry-go-round, on that cream-colored stallion. Rebecca! She swung round into sight. She rose, then descended, and Victor could see: She was naked. She just sat there, unclothed, her hands on the reins, as the horse climbed and fell as she circled. The blue ribbons in her hair were all she was wearing. Even through the rain on the window he could see her small breasts, her slim hips, and her legs wrapped around that wood stallion. Victor turned. He pressed his back to the wall. And he breathed. A strange chill descended his backbone. He turned once again to stare in, when he noticed the gentleman.

He was standing stark still by the wall. He was wearing a top hat and tail coat of linen. His back was to Victor; his face was invisible. But there was no mistaking that cane. It was topped with a carved ivory elephant head.

The man moved his arm and the music just stopped. It was suddenly gone. The carousel circled around once again. It was slowing. The steam had been cut. It slowed and then ground to a halt. The man approached the device with his hand out. He helped Rebecca climb down from the horse. Then he led her beside him, away from the carousel. She seemed tiny beside him. She seemed helpless and weak, and Victor's heart fairly burst from his chest. The man with the cane touched the wall and a panel gave way. It swung to the side. He stepped through the opening, drawing Rebecca behind him. The panel swept back into place, and they were suddenly gone. All that Victor could hear was the hissing of steam growing colder, and the interminable rush of the rain.

He stood there for several more minutes, his face pressed to the window, breathing hard. But no one appeared, no one came through the door or the panel. And the horses and unicorns and rabbits just sat there, immobile, grotesquely indifferent. Victor stood there and waited, and then finally gave up. His coat was soaked through. The collar felt icy and cold on his neck. He made his way back through the shrubbery toward the street. He squeezed through the fence. He walked back to the carriage and waited.

What could he do? he asked himself. He was simply her coachman. What was he meant to do?

He climbed back in the cab. He curled himself into the blanket, leaned back, and wrapped his arms around his chest. He sat there without moving for a long, long time. He sat there and waited and watched.

An hour later, the front door opened without warning. The butler stood framed by the light. Rebecca stood next to him. She was dressed in her blue woolen coat once again.

Victor saw her and leaped to his feet. He scrambled down to the pavement and hobbled as fast as he could to the gate. She was already out in the rain when he reached her.

The door slammed and the walkway grew dark. Victor put an arm around her shoulder, trying to shield Rebecca from the rain with his coat, but she just shrugged it off. She faced him and for the first time he noticed the tears in her eyes. Or was it the rain? he considered. Do blind eyes still cry? "Are you all right?" he asked. But she didn't answer.

When they got to the carriage, Rebecca climbed up by herself. She seemed determined to ascend unassisted. She curled up on the seat in the back.

Victor climbed up in the front. He kicked off the brake and the old horse, named Fortune, moved off with a shudder. He wanted to be home, to get out of the rain. He wanted all this to be over.

The streets were practically empty at this hour. It was still dark, but the air had that feeling about it, that light expectation that informed Victor sunrise was approaching. It would be dawn in an hour or two. The darkest part of the night was behind them.

"Did I ever tell you about my mother?" Rebecca's voice sounded deeper, as if she were getting a cold.

"No, I don't think so," he answered, although—of course— he was certain. Rebecca never talked of her past. With anyone. Among the cadgers, it was a source of great speculation.

"We came from Ireland five years ago. It was hard there," she said. "Not much food. Anyway, she met a man in Dublin, an Englishman. He wasn't my father," she added. There was something terribly sinister at the base of those words. He could feel it oozing up from beneath, like the slime of the red sod of Smithfield. "They were married and he moved us to London. We lived in a fairly nice house. On a nice street, not too far from Pimlico. In the Grosvenor estate. He worked for a shipping company. But things took a turn for the worse and one day he didn't come home. A week later he returned with a new Irish maid. My mother," she added, "my mother—she didn't last long after that. A Smithfield bargain he made of her."

"A what?" Victor asked, without turning. He couldn't look back at her face.

"A Smithfield bargain. It's when a husband sells his wife at the market. The buyer's usually a friend, some acquaintance or relative, generally driven by pity to see the union dissolve without rancor. That man," she continued. "That man put my mother in a halter, tied her up, right there, across from the Half Moon, in plain sight. By the gate of St. Bartholomew the Great." She released a small laugh. "Like a cow. A crowd gathered around and the auction began."

"I thought slavery was illegal," said Victor.

"Did you now? In the Indies it may be. If you're male. But a woman is naught but man's property. In the eyes of the law, she has no independence. Every stick, every brooch, the most intimate garment she wears, every armoire and chair is her husband's. So he sold her. My mother. My Moira. That was her name: Moira Finn. It means 'bitter and great' in old Celtic. She was both." Rebecca took a deep breath. "Strangely enough, things looked up for a while after that. My mother was pretty, you see. She had precious few skills but her eyes were alluring and her figure was neat. The men fancied her and she pleased them. It seems long ago now. Don't be shocked."

"I'm not shocked."

He heard a low laugh. "You may be older in years, but I've seen more."

"You might be surprised," answered Victor.

But Rebecca ignored him. She was trapped in her story. "My mother was helpless, you see," she continued. "All alone in the city, with hardly a friend and no family. She had little choice. She met a young man who turned out to be rich, but he refused to see her in public. And besides, he soon tired of her. There were others, of course. Many others. She began to work nights, wearing red in St. James's. Then the theater bars down Drury Lane. Next she moved on to Lisle and the Haymarket, and the Colonnade where Regent Street curves into Piccadilly. When she hailed down a john, she'd use one of the rooms in the shopping arcade, right above from some milliner's shop."

Rebecca laughed. It was an alien sound. It didn't belong in her mouth. Victor resisted an urge to pull over.

"Sometimes I wonder if the people below us, shopping late, in those expensive and fine trinket stores, if they knew what was happening above them, right there, but a few feet away. Such gay goings-on," she continued.

"You were present?"

"Sometimes. I had to be somewhere. And it was better than being at home, with her suitors." She sighed.

"You don't have to tell me all this," Victor said. "It's not really necessary."

"But I want to," she said. "I don't know why, but I trust you, Victor. And I have to tell somebody."

Victor didn't reply. He let her continue her story.

"Over time, as the powder and paint failed to cover, things grew progressively worse. We moved several times—from the Haymarket to Vauxhall, to the Cremorne Gardens, to a one-room along Edgware Road. My mother started to drink and it was many a day I was forced to undress her and put her to bed. She got sick." Her voice broke for a moment. Then she laughed once again, that odd little laugh with no center. "By the time we were living in Dockland, you could have had her for a tumbler of gin, right there, in an alley, up against some brick wall. If you'd wanted," she added. "But few did. I found her one day on the stoop of our building. She had fallen asleep on the stairs in the snow. She had fallen asleep there, and died."

For a time, neither of them spoke. They just sat there in silence as Fortune continued, as they clip-clopped along down the road. Then she said, "My mother introduced me to the Master the night I turned twelve. On my birthday. I'll never forget it, for as long as I live. But I love her. Still, Victor, to this day. No matter what happened. I have to love her. There are some things that happen. Things that aren't really fair, or deserved. Things that hurt. And you try to pretend that they don't mean a thing. They don't matter. Or that they never occurred in the first place. You find ways of concealing them. From the world. From yourself. You tuck them away, but you can't, can you, Victor."

"I don't know what you mean."

"Yes, you do. I can tell. You and I, we're the same. There's a hole deep inside us. In our hearts, or what's left of them. There's a void, Victor. Like a cave where our screams keep on echoing. I may be blind. And you may be crippled. We may hail from opposite ends of the earth. But we share the same pain, you and I. The same wound, Victor. Maybe that's why I trust you."

"What happened back there, at the mansion?"

Rebecca didn't respond. Victor could no longer stop himself. He turned and looked at her, like Orpheus at Eurydice. He had no choice. Rebecca had curled herself into a ball in the blanket. Her face was all he could see. It looked fragile and pale in the lamplight. Like an orbitless moon. She stared back at him, sightless, and said, "Do we have to go back right away?"

Victor shook his head, as if she could see him. "No," he said. "We don't have to do anything. Where do you want to go?"

"I don't care," she replied. "Just keep driving. Drive until the road stops. I don't care where we go, Victor, just as long as you're with me."

"Anywhere?"

"To a little cottage in the country. Far, far away from the cadging and Dicity. With a field for the planting in back. And a room for two young ones upstairs. And a great open sky, Victor, full of stars and a moon. A sky that goes on for eternity. Promise me, Victor. Someday. Just the two of us. Promise me."

"I promise," he said, and he meant it.

· CHAPTER · 10

VICTOR AND REBECCA never spoke about their trip into Mayfair after that, and the Master never asked the boy to drive her there again. Perhaps he didn't trust their growing friendship. But there were many other errands on which Victor was dispatched, and some were equally repugnant. The Master was impressed with Victor's mastery of horses, and the boy became his favorite coachman. On occasion, he'd loan the boy out to associates and friends. One time, at the tail end of February, as winter grew more frigid, Victor was instructed to chauffeur Tipple and Biggs about the city in Master Hartley's wagon.

They started in the early morning. Tipple and Biggs lived next door to one another in a particularly seedy, tumbledown section of London called Paradise Row. Unlit and reeking of human and animal dung, Paradise Row lay behind a smallpox hospital, a mile and a half northeast of Covent Garden. As soon as Victor arrived with the wagon, the two men emerged from Tipple's cottage bearing a laundry hamper. With great difficulty—for the basket was obviously heavy—they heaved the hamper up into the wagon and instructed Victor to "drive steady but deliberate, as if nothing's about." Victor tickled Fortune with the tip of his whip and the gelding made off. Tipple seemed to be in a particularly sullen mood that morning. It was clear from the few sentences he spoke to Biggs that he wasn't very happy with their current working situation.

"This better make hay," he said, blowing his nose. He was suffering from a bad cold. "I needs bees and honey."

"You should have spent the harry lime with me and the coke last night, Mr. Tipple, with a nice Jack surpass of some finger-and-thumb, if you please. A touch of the broads ain't what's needed," said Biggs.

In the time that Victor had spent in London, he'd picked up more than a phrase or two of the local Cockney dialect; Biggs was chiding Tipple for playing cards—pronounced *cords*, which rhymed with *broads*—instead of sharing a glass of rum—or finger-and-thumb—with his friends.

Tipple didn't respond. He was too busy blowing his nose with great force in his tatty blue handkerchief.

Their destination was King's College. Victor pulled up by the entrance and the two men jumped off hastily and removed the laundry hamper. It was then that Victor finally saw what they carried. The basket tipped over as they lowered it, grunting and heaving, by the door. The lid fell open and a hand slipped out, and then an arm, and then the rancid torso of some man who had spent some time already in the earth. They popped the body back into the hamper and rang the bell. A few minutes later, a man wearing an apron appeared at the door. He was short, with a mop of coal black hair, and a scar on his left cheek. He looked out at Tipple and Biggs, at their hamper, and told them to enter. Victor waited outside for a good half an hour before they reappeared. Tipple seemed somewhat more pleased now, less moody. They picked up another hamper—empty, this time—near the entrance. They tossed it up in the wagon and leaped in beside it. "LBA," Mr. Biggs said. "At Gower and Euston."

LBA was a euphemism for a church of the Baptist persuasion, LBA standing for London Baptist Association. Victor hastened off toward Euston Square. He knew the area quite well. It was not far from Hatton Garden, Saffron Hill, and the other streets leading northward off Holborn in the section of London called "Little Italy," due to the high number of immigrants. It was proximate to Clerkenwell, where clock and instrument makers resided, which proved useful to those who earned a living playing barrel organs. Victor sometimes went there in the evenings for a bite to eat on his way home, after a good day of begging. He liked to stuff himself with pasta and nostalgic cutlets, with the victuals of Po. But he always regretted it later, for the food had grown too rich for his stomach.

When they finally arrived, Victor noticed some sort of funeral service going on; the street was busy with men and women in mourning clothes. Tipple told him to wait as they unloaded the basket and made their way along a long dark alley at the back of the church. Fifteen minutes later, the two men returned at a run. "Be quick, boy," said Tipple as they heaved the hamper up on the wagon. "We 'ave company."

Victor looked down the alley and saw a small crowd of men gathering by the church door. They pointed at Tipple and Biggs and gave chase. Victor brandished the whip and Fortune moved off, breaking into a trot, then a canter. They coursed down the street, made a left, then a right. Victor noticed the last of his pursuers in the distance. They were waving their arms. They were shouting. Then they vanished round the corner and Tipple and Biggs began to laugh and pat each other on the back.

"A job well done, Mr. Biggs," said Tipple.

"Right you are, then, Mr. Tipple. You too, lad. Your bee hivin's robin."

Victor nodded and pulled back on the reins. *Bee hiving* meant driving; *robin hood* stood for good. He felt both flattered and terribly ashamed, for he knew what reclined in that hamper in back.

They stopped once more at King's College to drop off their load, and then Tipple told Victor to drive on to Biltspur, to a pub called the Naked Boy, although it was barely past nine in the morning. Victor knew the pub. It was not far from Smithfield, across from St. Bartholomew's Hospital.

When they arrived, Tipple and Biggs went inside while Victor tended to the wagon and Fortune. Despite the hour, the pub was quite busy, half-filled already with patrons. Some breakfasted on sausages and spuds, some on steak and kidney pies. Victor wondered at the crowd. It appeared that most of them had been up all night, and were stopping off for a meal and a pint before bed. He studied the faces of the men as he walked to the rear of the tavern to join Tipple and Biggs. They were a rough lot, to be sure. Some chatted raucously—those who'd imbibed to excess, Victor thought—but most ate without speaking, or drank their rum or their gin or their beer with odd furtive looks round the pub. The Naked Boy was a flash house: not merely a pub, but a place to fence stolen goods.

Victor sat down and they ordered a bottle of rum and three glasses.

"I don't drink," said the boy.

"You do now," Tipple answered. "You're one of the lads."

Biggs reached out and grabbed him, and squeezed him. "One of us. A true Resurrection Man."

"A what?"

"Why, what we are," said Tipple as a boy approached with their rum. Tipple took the bottle and poured out three shots in the glasses. "To us," he continued. "And especially to you, Mr. Biggs."

"No, to you, Mr. Tipple." And they touched their two glasses together.

"Look about you," said Tipple to Victor. "You see all these men? The Boy is a friend to the snatcher." Then Tipple explained.

In this great age of medical discovery, physicians hungered for bodies to dissect so they could unravel the mysteries of human anatomy. But—other than the cadavers of executed criminals, which were few and far between—such bodies were illegal to procure. Body-snatchers took advantage of this demand to dig up corpses from unguarded graves. They izzied bodies from church halls and undertakers, as Tipple and Biggs had done that very morning. They masqueraded as kin, and kept vigil at poorhouses and hospitals as the moribund crept toward the grave. A man could earn eight to twelve guineas for a single fresh corpse, around half of what a factory boy earned in a year, or a workingman over three months. It was lucrative work, and not particularly dangerous. Peelers had more pressing issues about which to worry, and the Charlies who guarded the churchyards were generally old and incompetent.

"Why do you think we stuffed you in that coffin, Master Victor, on our journey from Portsmouth to London?"

"I don't know. I asked Nico but he wouldn't tell me. And the cadgers don't talk about you, Mr. Tipple. They say it's bad luck. About you or the man with the cane."

Tipple leaned back and laughed. His toothless gums glimmered in the lamplight. "I don't wonder," he said. "I feel flattered. We're legends, we are, Mr. Biggs."

"Rightly famous," said Biggs as he lifted his glass. Tipple poured him another.

"Drink up, Master Victor. I fancy some cows in a paddock for breakfast."

This meant haddock, of course.

"And I wants to shew you somethin'. Drink up, boy, you'll need it."

Victor drank his rum down in one gulp. He could feel the liquor warming his face.

"If you wants to get out of the street, we could use a sound hand on the reins." Tipple reached down beside him. He began to untie a small bag from his belt. "If yer willin' and able." He dropped the bag on the table. It was made out of cowhide. Tipple undid the thong at the top. He lifted it up, turned it over, and something slipped out. It fell on the table and rolled.

Teeth, Victor realized. Half a jawbone. And shockingly fresh, for they glistened with blood. He could still see small pieces of mushroomy flesh on the side of the bone. Like a mold. Victor turned away. The rum roiled in his pharynx. The teeth and the jawbone were human.

"Do you ken what this is?" Tipple asked him.

"It's a jaw and some teeth," Victor answered, still looking away. "Freshly pulled, I would wager."

"It's two quid, boy," said Tipple.

"Or more," added Biggs. "And expertly pulled, with an awl—no mean feat, Master Victor. Why, a surgeon couldn't have done it more neatly. You're an artist, Mr. Tipple."

"It's a warm meal and bed, boy," added Tipple, ignoring his friend. "And a flagon of finger-and-thumb." He lifted his glass. He winked and slurped down his drink. "What say you, Master Victor? Are you with us?"

"I'd rather beg, if you please, Mr. Tipple."

"What's that?" said Biggs. He leaned a bit closer. The folds of his chest pillowed over the table. "Are you daft, boy? Mr. Tipple 'ere is extendin' 'is 'and. Look upon it with seriousness, boy, and respect." He grabbed Victor by the head. He swiveled his face. Tipple was holding his hand out, reaching out to him. His fingers hovered over the table.

"Take it," said Tipple. Then he opened his hand. A half crown slipped from his fingers and fell on the jawbone. The coin bounced on the upper incisors and settled. "You've earned it."

Victor looked at the coin. It glimmered and shone. Two and sixpence was a great deal of money, but he couldn't reach out. He just couldn't, though he longed to.

"As you wish," Tipple said, retrieving his money. "Off you go then. Back to Fortune." He gathered the teeth up as well. "If you fancy the life of a cadger, far be it from me to deny you." He stuffed the jaw in his bag. "As Biggs here said, Victor, your bee hivin's robin. You can drive for your crust, on a comfortable seat, high and free, or hobble about like the cripple you be."

Victor stood up. He gathered his crutch and looked down at the men. "I am what I am, Mr. Tipple," he said. "Nothing more, nothing less. What you see, sir. Not that I don't value your most generous offer. But I'll never be what I'm not. It's not in me."

Tipple nodded and gummed a small smile.

Biggs gave Victor a poke. "We all crawl on God's earth in our own way, Master Victor," he said. "One does what one has to, until the last reckonin'. To the hangman," he added, as he lifted his glass.

"To the hangman, Mr. Biggs," rejoined Tipple. Once again they threw back their glasses. "After all," he continued. "We provide a valuable service to the scientific community."

"Right you are, Mr. Tipple." Biggs poured two more shots. "To the scientific community," he added, raising his glass.

"The scientific community."

"I'll meet you outside," Victor said, hobbling off. He weaved his way back through the crowd. He stopped at the door and looked over his shoulder. Tipple and Biggs were still drinking. They were still pouring out shots and tossing them back with abandon.

He hobbled along to the wagon. It was pleasure and paining

again; it was raining, Victor noticed. He patted Fortune on the side of the neck. He said a few words and climbed back to his seat. Then he sat there and waited and watched, a blanket wrapped round him, covering his head. He waited and watched through the window as Tipple and Biggs had their breakfast of liquor.

This was how most of the children spent their evenings, assuming their day had been fruitful. The Naked Boy was a true public house, but since the new Beerhouse Act of the previous year, thousands of new retailers had sprung up all over the city. Tiny shops and even the front rooms of dwellings could be converted for the price of a license, and the ensuing competition between public and beerhouse drove the price of a beer ever cheaper. It was no wonder everyone drank, Victor thought. How else could they drown out the foul stench of London, their grimy existence, their menial jobs, that slatternly wench and that nerve-wracking gaggle of children they came home to each night? And because the beer was often diluted, proprietors concealed the weakness by doctoring it with the poisonous *Cocculus indicus*, a berry grown in Ceylon, which had the effect of increasing its potency. A workingman, earning his fifteen to thirty shillings a week, drank a mere pint a day, but this cost one and tuppence a week. Some families spent twenty percent of their income on drink. And that was at home. According to Nico, there were more than seven thousand retailers of alcohol in the city, one for every three hundred people. A beerhouse or pub could be found, on the average, every one hundred yards. Annual consumption was in excess of twenty gallons a head, or about three pints a week for every man, woman, and child in the country. And that was excepting the teetotalers—the thousands upon thousands in the Evangelical and Methodist movements.

Victor had tried drinking. From time to time, his parents in Modena had passed him a glass of Barolo at dinner. He knew most of the children drank beer, and many drank spirits like gin. But he found the taste horrible. And he'd never enjoyed the sensation of being so out of control, of losing his grip on reality. It made you too vulnerable, or Dutch drunk, unreasonably brave. He'd seen what liquor had done to the old man in Portsmouth, and he remembered what Rebecca had said of her mother. So he waited and watched as Tipple and Biggs grew increasingly drunker. When they'd finally finished their meal, they slithered their way through the crowd and staggered outside to the street. Victor shouted their names as they clung to each other, as they stared at the sky, the rain washing their faces. Then they turned and they saw him, and returned—arm in arm—to the wagon.

"After you, Mr. Tipple," said Biggs with a flourish. "Up you go, then."

"You're a gent," Tipple answered. He hoisted himself up with great effort. Victor gave him a hand. "And you too, Master Victor. Though a half-wit, like Nico. A fool."

"There you go, Mr. Tipple," said Victor.

Tipple tripped and sat down in the back. "Nothing to it," he said.

Biggs climbed in beside him. The wagon tilted and sagged from his copious weight. "Home, coachman," he cried, pointing wildly.

Victor made a little clicking noise and Fortune plodded off down the street. The drive to Paradise Row was surprisingly painless. The streets were packed already, with carts and carriages, with foot traffic, milling crowds, and the odd pig or drunk, lying in the sewer in the center of the street. Sweepers and beggars paraded about. Some Victor knew. But despite the congestion, the driving was pleasant, for Tipple and Biggs had grown silent at last. They had fallen asleep—at the slightest vibration—as soon as the wagon had pulled away from the curb. They lay cheek to cheek on the boards in the back, clinging together like drowned sailors: Biggs bloated and huge, with his little round head, and Tipple with his long gangly legs and cadaverous torso. They completed each other, like a chair and an ottoman, like the line and the dot of an i.

Thankfully, Biggs woke as they rounded the corner into Paradise Row. Perhaps it was the powerful aroma of the street, the livid open wound of the sewer; or the shouting and screaming coming from the various doorways, crowded with women and children, the odd man. Perhaps it was the smell of beer and vomit stained with beer that made him quiver, then wake, then sit up and look round.

"Get up, Mr. Tipple," he said. "I see the gates of Rome." Which meant, of course, they were home.

They managed to help each other out of the wagon and to stagger to their cottages. They opened their front doors at precisely the same time, turned, and stared at one another. They tipped their hats in unison.

"G'day, Mr. Tipple," said Biggs.

"G'day, Mr. Biggs," replied Tipple.

Then they were gone and Victor breathed easy. As casual and indifferent as he tried to appear, he always felt nervous around Tipple and Biggs. And it wasn't because they had stuffed him into that coffin the very first time they had met. It wasn't the jawbone which Tipple had dropped on the table in the Naked Boy. Nor was it the fact that they were Resurrection Men, that they dug up the dead to sell parts for dissection. It was something innate, or—more chilling still—something that should have been present at the heart of their being but that was strangely removed, somehow missing, left out. And the absence was growing, for the void was inexorably eating away at the boundaries that held them together. Lines most men would never cross were dissolving within Tipple and Biggs, like a Screaver's appeal on the pavement, worn away by the passage of feet. They didn't belong. They lived outside the law and the ordinary limits of men. They were like penguins, like birds in a maritime world. They flew in the sea with their own personal aerodynamics.

Victor ran a few more errands for the Master on his way back to St. Giles. He had almost made it home when he saw Nico pelting down the street. The boy appeared frantic with fear. Two men ran behind him, pushing and shoving, trailing his wake. And they looked angry.

Victor cried out to him and Nico glanced up. He dashed through the street toward the wagon. The men were catching up. Nico skipped, ran, and leaped through the air. He seemed to hang there, in space, for eternity. Then he fell to the boards and rolled over. He struggled to hang on to the wagon. The road was blessedly clear. Victor exhorted old Fortune, cracked the whip by the old gelding's ears. The horse bolted and galloped still faster. Pedestrians scurried away. The two men tried to keep up, but Victor soon lost them. They grew winded and stopped. Victor could see them. They stood there and stared, simply panting, as the two boys retreated from sight.

After another quarter mile, Victor finally slowed down and pulled over. He maneuvered the wagon down a serpentine alley. It was full of refuse, rotten vegetables, and the skins of some unidentifiable animals. Victor kicked on the break. "Are you hurt?" he inquired, finally turning around.

Nico stood up in the back of the wagon. He brushed at his clothes. He settled the tricolor hat on his head, the one that Victor had given him. *Mille grazie,* " he said, and then turned to jump off.

"Wait," Victor said, in Italian. "What happened? Who were they?"

"Who?"

"Those men. Don't be sly, Nico. They were chasing you."

"I was asleep, in an alley, when they woke me. They were tying me up with a rope."

"Tying you up? Why? What for?"

The boy didn't answer.

"I think I recognize one of them," Victor said. "The one with the hat. I could swear I saw him in the Naked Boy just this morning."

"They're not Resurrection Men. They're worse."

"Worse? What do you mean, worse? What could be worse?"

"When they catch you, you never come back."

Victor tried to press him further, but Nico had lost his direction. Like a butterfly, his mind had alighted and was drifting away. He stared into space. He turned and looked up at Victor, and then smiled. "I must go now," he said. All his fear and anxiety had suddenly vanished. "Time to beg." He jumped off the back of the wagon.

Victor watched as Nico skipped down the alley, growing ever smaller and smaller, more distant as he gradually retreated, until he turned around the corner and vanished.

Victor sighed and sat back on his seat. One day, he thought, he wouldn't be there to save him, and Nico would vanish for good, simply never come home, like the hundreds and thousands of others who went missing each year. Victor clicked his tongue and Fortune moved off with a whinny.

·CHAPTER·
II

IT WAS STRANGE, Victor thought, some time later, how the smallest thing, the most capricious decision, sometimes made the profoundest of differences. One time, he had seen one of the cadgers take a step off the pavement, for no reason at all, put one foot in the street for a moment, only to be struck by a carriage and crushed. On another occasion, he'd been asked to share in a half dozen whelks by a friend of Rebecca's, but refused since he hadn't the time. Then, upon returning to the house in the evening, he'd found the girl lying in a heap on the floor, moaning and puking from food poisoning. She had died without fanfare later that night. One might take a left or a right at a corner, or go straight, and walk right into Dicity. One might say "Yes" or say "No" to a friend's invitation for a flagon of finger-and-thumb, and end up cut open in the back of an alley. It was fortune, or luck, or your fate, as some of the children would have it. Call it kismet or karma, it was only a few days following his journey with Tipple and Biggs that an event occurred which was to change Victor's life in ways he could never have foreseen at the time. He was fixing the wing of a barn owl with Nico, wrapping up the soiled bandages in an intricate webbing of knots—just as the old man in Portsmouth had shown him—when Rebecca swept in through the door. "Where ya' cadging, today, Master Victor?" she said.

"I don't know. Between the Strand and the Garden, perhaps. It's been cozy with ladies of late. Or down by the river. Why?" He tightened the last strap of the bandages. The owl cocked its head, tried to fly. "Easy, boy," Victor said, trying to calm it.

"Do you mind if I join you?" she asked.

The owl pecked at his arm. Victor thrust his right forearm up, and then out, into the owl's tiny chest. "Step up," he said. The owl mounted his arm. It lifted its wing as if to test the new bandages. "You'll live," Victor said.

"Well, do you?"

"What's that? No, of course not." Then he turned. "What's the matter?" he asked her.

Rebecca looked at her shoes.

"Ever since Mary went missing," he continued, "you've been acting peculiar. She'll turn up, just you wait. She's gone missin' before, has she not?"

"On occasion." Rebecca looked up and he noticed the fear in her eyes. "There are rumors about," she continued. "I'd just rather not be alone, not today. It's such a fine day, Master Victor."

"As you wish," he replied as he slipped the bird back in its cage. The bird fluttered its wings. It blinked and it turned, resting its head on its shoulders. "But keep a fair distance, if you please, or you'll sodden my cadging."

They made their way from the house in St. Giles and walked west toward the Strand. It was indeed a beautiful day. The sun had finally emerged from the smog and every rooftop in London glistened and glimmered, shimmered with dew. A cool but not unpleasant breeze washed through the streets, blowing the ill scents of the city away. The linens and silks of the gentlefolk seemed particularly resplendent this morning. The air bestowed a bright frivolity upon all who ventured abroad. The sunlight had awakened the city, and her citizens took advantage of the fickle brightness to take a turn or two around the block. All walked with an alien lightness, as if buoyed by the sudden luminosity. Victor reveled in these mornings. They generally brought plump cadging. For as the blood quickened, so did the fingers. Who could begrudge a farthing to a starving beggar on a day such as this? Who wouldn't tarry, for a moment at least, for some seconds in the enlivening sunlight, to examine an owl? Victor couldn't have selected a more suitable foil. On a day of such pitiless brightness, the sight of an owl in a cage seemed absurd, almost oxymoronic. Especially trussed up as it was, with that sling.

Victor had been standing on his corner for about an hour when he noticed the man. He had seen him several times before, on other days, always staring out that same small window on the second landing, just across the way. The man never said a thing. He simply sat there and stared. But this day was different. Perhaps it was the air, the sunlight and the vibrant jostling of the busy street. Perhaps it was pure chance. But this day, the man gazed down upon the boulevard, at Victor and his owl, and then suddenly disappeared. A moment later he was standing by a side door in the street. Victor watched him as he waited for a carriage to idle by. Then he made his way through the crowd, hopping ungraciously across the open sewers, and dashed to Victor.

"You there," he began, a tad out of breath.

Victor looked him over. He was an elderly gentleman, dressed in a lime-green silk waistcoat and dark umber cutaway. A creamy gold kerchief bubbled up from one sleeve like the head of a beer. He had bright turquoise eyes, handsome and clear, almost emerald-colored, and a delicate mouth. His hair and his sideburns were startlingly white. "That barn owl," he said, pointing a skeletal finger.

"Yes, sir," said Victor. This following part was particularly crucial, and he stared at the gentleman. The old man's next gesture, his next sentence, would inform all of Victor's behavior. The boy would become either piteous or shrill, gregarious or taciturn, endearing or duly pathetic. But the gentleman took him by surprise. He barely looked at Victor. He stared, instead, at the owl. "Who bandaged your bird up?" he asked, after a moment of scrutiny.

"Why, I did," said Victor. And he became himself.

"Is that so? And who taught you to doctor that way?"

Victor stepped up. He put his crutch on the ground and lifted the cage. "It seemed like the right thing to do."

"Indeed," said the gentleman. He looked down at Victor. "And why's that?" he inquired, raising a brow. "I mean, why did you wrap it around in that manner?"

"That's how the muscle sits, sir, on the breastbone."

"What of it? It's the wing that's been broken."

"But the muscles at the shoulder need to compensate, sir, and so they pull on the chest. It's all of a piece, sir. One great blanket of muscle. Or a quilt."

"You're a student of medicine, then, are you?" The old man took a step backward and laughed. "What's your name, boy?"

"Victor."

"Victor what?"

"Just Victor."

"I see," said the gentleman. "Haven't I seen you standing about here before?"

"Yes, sir. I've seen you. In your window on the second landing." Victor pointed across the street.

"So you have. That's my house."

"And a fine house it is, sir."

The gentleman laughed. "Where are you from, Victor?" he asked him.

"I live in St. Giles."

"No, before that."

"Near Portsmouth."

"Where were you born, boy? What city?"

"In Modena, Emilia-Romagna. Not far from Bologna."

The gentleman nodded. He pointed at the crutch in the street. "And that affliction, does it ever hurt?"

"Sometimes."

"Mmm. To be sure," said the gentleman. He took a step closer to Victor. Then, without warning, he reached out and began to run a hand down the boy's crippled leg.

Victor pulled back. "What are you doing?" he said. Just then Rebecca drew near.

"What's happening?" she asked as she sensed his alarm.

The gentleman straightened and turned. "And what have we here?" he responded, confronting the girl. "A traveling companion?"

"Who are you?" asked Rebecca.

"Please, excuse me," he said, "I've forgotten my manners. My daughter is always chiding me for that. That, and for smoking too much. And for not eating my greens. And for . . . I tend to forget myself at times. The name's Quigley. Doctor Thomas H. Quigley. I'm a physician."

"And your interest in Victor, what is it?"

The man smiled. "Purely a medical one, I assure you. Why, you're blind, aren't you?" he said, like an afterthought.

"You are indeed a man of science, Doctor Quigley."

"Forgive me," he said, "but how long have you been blind?"

"Since I was born," she replied.

"And your friend here. How long has he been . . . you know . . . crippled?"

"Why don't you ask him yourself? He speaks English."

"Indeed," he replied, glancing back at the boy. "When did you break your leg, Victor? How did it happen?"

Victor put the cage down on the pavement. "I fell," he said flatly. "Some months ago. I don't remember exactly."

"How would you like to come back to my house for some crumpets and tea? I live right over there."

"Yes, I know," Victor said. "We both know where you live."

The man chuckled. "So you said. Well, how about it?" he added.

"Why?"

"Well, to be honest," he said, "I've been watching you, Victor. Out my window. I've seen you begging here in this same spot for some weeks. And I've noticed the way that you move. I've watched you, and I've come to the conclusion that, perhaps, there's a chance I can help you."

"Help me? Why? How?"

"Why? Well, I'm sure I don't know. For the challenge, I suppose. But let's not get ahead of ourselves. I'll have to examine you first, Victor, check the bones in your leg."

"I have no money," said Victor.

"Consider yourself fortunate. For then you have no in-laws, no well-wishers, and no hangers-on. Come along, lad. Bring your owl, if you wish. And your friend, if she cares to."

Victor hesitated, but Rebecca started after the gentleman.

"How do you know we can trust him?" Victor asked in a whisper.

"He's all right. Don't fret, I can tell."

"How can you tell? You're . . ."

"I'm what? Untroubled by sight? Is that what you were going to say? The eyes lie, Victor, but the voice echoes up from the heart." With that she turned and made her way across the street, behind the old man.

Victor followed. They entered the side door into the gentleman's house. And what a house it was! Victor was stupefied. In all his years—save for that glimpse of that mansion in Mayfair—Victor had never seen anything like it. At Rebecca's insistence, he described what he saw. The back hall led into a kitchen with a great roaring fire where a fat goose was cooking deliberately. To one side stood a coal-heated copper of ample proportions, embedded in stone, with a great iron lid. On the other was a sink and slop bucket, crowned by row upon row of wood shelving stuffed with colorful platters and plates. Victor made his way toward the table when the gentleman motioned him forward.

"No, in here," said the doctor. He beckoned and the two children followed. They moved down the hall past a sizeable dining room. It was opulent beyond reason. A gas chandelier made of glass or lead crystal bloomed from the ceiling. The dining table was at least eight feet long, topped with a blue satin runner. Still-lifes studded the walls: mostly dead birds, or fall fruit. The physician kept moving. They made their way past numerous rooms, each equally splendid: a music room with a grand pianoforte; a library with thousands of books; a sitting room; a cloakroom . . . the house seemed to go on forever.

"A four-figure man," said Rebecca to Victor discreetly. "A man of great means."

The doctor finally paused by a set of closed doors. He turned with a wink and pulled them apart. It was his study or office, guessed Victor. The room was quite small compared to the others he'd seen, but cozy and warm. A fire blazed in the hearth. There was a small walnut desk with a pair of chairs facing it. There was a padded red leather settee. And beyond was a globe of the world, made of wood, three feet in diameter, and a cherry wood cabinet topped with decanters. Books lined the rear wall. Dr. Quigley motioned the children to enter. "Sit there," he said gruffly to Victor. "On that leather bench." He pointed to the settee.

Victor hobbled over, propped his crutch against the wall, and sat down. "If you please, sir," he said. "You mentioned some crumpets and tea." At three shillings a pound, tea was a luxury ill afforded by beggars. And Victor was hungry. He hadn't eaten all day.

The physician laughed. "Don't worry, lad. I promised you tea and you'll have it. But let me examine your leg first."

Dr. Quigley moved over to the red settee. He asked Victor to remove his trousers and the boy did so without embarrassment. Despite himself, Quigley gasped as he spied Victor's leg. It was twisted and gnarled as a willow branch. Bone bulged from beneath, as if some part of him were trying to escape through the skin. Though sightless, Rebecca averted her gaze.

After a few minutes, Dr. Quigley patted Victor on the head and said, "It's not so bad. Believe me, I've seen worse."

"Can you help me?" asked Victor.

The doctor shrugged. Then he nodded and said, "Yes, I think so. If you'd like. I can help you, but . . ."

"But what?"

"It will not be pleasant. The only way to help you is to rebreak the long bones. All three of them: the femur, tibia, and fibula. I have some laudanum and rum, but, to be frank, you'll probably feel it. I daren't give you too much."

"And if you do," said Victor. "If you succeed, will I be able to walk again? Without a crutch, I mean?"

"That's what I'm hoping. On the other hand, the procedure could just make it worse. There's a chance—although slight—that such an operation will cause an infection. In that case, you could lose your leg."

"Don't do it," said Rebecca. "Better a bad leg than no leg at all."

Victor looked up at the girl. She had grown wan. Here eyes were brimming with tears. He looked at the doctor.

Quigley smiled. Then he shrugged and said, "It's up to you."

"When could you do this?" asked Victor.

"No time like the present," said Quigley. He looked at Rebecca.

"You mean right now? Today?" she replied. "You should take some time to consider it, Victor. At least overnight."

Perhaps fearing that the boy might never return, the doctor began to remove his brown cutaway. "I have other patients to see. It's now, boy, or never. As you please."

Victor glanced back at Rebecca. "If there's a chance," he said. "No matter how small."

Rebecca looked deflated. She bowed her head, turned away.

Dr. Quigley moved off to the cherry wood cabinet in the corner. He reached inside and removed a small dark blue bottle. Moments later he returned to the settee. Carefully, he poured out a few drops of liquid into a glass. Then he filled it with rum from a nearby decanter. "Drink this," he insisted.

Victor took the glass and consumed it without taking a breath. He winced from the taste of the alcohol. "How long before . . ."

"Not long," Quigley said. "Just lay there. Be still. Try and rest."

Victor reclined on the bench. He watched as the doctor walked back to his desk. Quigley fumbled about in a drawer. When he returned to the settee, he was carrying a mallet and chisel. "I don't yet feel the . . ." Victor couldn't finish. His head had grown suddenly heavy. The room darkened, as if a cloud had just passed by the sun. He felt as though he were in that coffin again, as if the world were shrinking around him, growing progressively smaller. "Rebecca," he said. "Rebecca, are you there?"

Rebecca moved closer. He could see her face float in the air right above him. She was smiling. She was holding him down by the shoulders. "I'm here," she said. She brought her face close. "You're a brave boy, Victor. Do you know that?"

"No, I'm not. I'm afraid." Victor tried to sit up, but the doctor restrained him.

"Keep him still," Quigley said. "Just a minute."

Victor watched as the doctor bound his chest and his stomach and legs with three sets of straps. He seemed to rise nonetheless, to course out of his skin, and to hover there, just out of reach, immediately above his own form. He watched as Quigley placed the chisel to his leg. "I can't, Rebecca. Tell him to stop," Victor said. "Let me go, doctor. Don't . . ."

The mallet arched upward, then down in a stuttering cascade. Victor saw it connect. He heard a sharp crack, like a branch underfoot, like the parting of pond ice. The sound seemed to travel inside him. It was followed by pain, a white lancing agony that pulsed through his leg, through his stomach and into his head. Victor screamed, but the noise was cut short. It was caught as Rebecca leaned over him, as she pressed her warm lips against his. The scream rushed from his mouth into hers, inflating her cheeks, where it grew still and withered, and died. Like a flower. Like a dream. Like a lozenge of longing.

"I love you," she said, or was it the rum and the laudanum? Victor couldn't be sure. The words settled inside him, like stars in an infinite sky.

PART III

·CHAPTER· 12

B E QUICK, MAN," said Lambro. "He's bleeding all over the place."

Colonel Henry Maxwell leaned over the table and dabbed up the blood that seeped from the deep laceration in the boy's open chest. "I'm trying, but this rag's fairly soaked."

"Get another one," said the doctor. He pointed his chin at a pile of loose garments. "I'm afraid we may lose him. Good God!" he exclaimed.

Colonel Maxwell picked up a torn towel and dashed over to help him. "What is it?" he said.

Lambro lifted his hands. They were livid with blood. He wiped his brow with the sleeve of his shirt. "The pericardium," he answered. "It's swollen. I fear that it's filling with blood. There. You see?"

Maxwell leaned over the table. He couldn't discern one pulpy mass from the next.

"His heart beats in that vessel. There," Lambro said.

The colonel peered in the opening. The bag of raw flesh at which the doctor was pointing was pulsing and seething with life. "Yes, I see it."

"A blood vessel must have burst. If we don't drain the pericardial sac, he'll die. But I've never attempted it."

"Steady, man."

"Bring the lamp closer."

The colonel complied. "How will you . . ."

"I don't know. Fetch me that awl, by the sink."

The colonel went over and plucked out the pointed device. It had a short wooden handle and a long metal point. It was used to make punctures in leather. He brought it back to the doctor.

"Put it into the flame of the lamp. There. That's right."

Maxwell toasted the end of the awl. Then he passed it to Lambro and the doctor inserted the tip through the pericardium wall. A fountain of blood burst out through his fingers, filling the cavity.

"Mop it up," Lambro said. "There you go. It's subsiding." The doctor bent over. He examined the heart chamber. "The swelling's retreating. Thank heavens." He plucked another feather from the pheasant and stripped it of its barbs. Then, with great care and concentration, he cut another small hole in the boy's right side and placed the naked feather through the opening. Now, two plumes poked out of the boy's skin: one to bleed the air out of the chest cavity; the other to drain the blood which still dripped from the pericardium and made its way across the lung into the cavity. "We haven't much time," he continued. "The boy's lost a great deal of blood. I've done what I can."

"What now?" Maxwell asked him.

"Time to sew him together." He tugged at the loose flaps of skin. "And to pray."

Dr. Lambro worked quickly and efficiently. The needle and thread fairly flew. "Like sewing canvas," he said.

Colonel Maxwell looked horrified. "But this sail is alive."

"Let's hope that he lives out the hour," said Lambro. The more he worked, the less blood there was to clean up. Eventually the cavity disappeared altogether.

Colonel Maxwell reached out for the bottle of rum which he'd placed on a stool by the fire. It was his third slug of liquor in only ten minutes. "Then what happened?" he said. "To the beggar you knew."

Dr. Lambro glanced up. "You mean Victor?"

"Aye," he said. "You left him pretty much as this boy, save under that mallet and chisel. Did Quigley succeed? Did he walk? And what of Rebecca and the rest of the children?" He sat on the stool by the fire. "What happened?"

"Yes, he walked," Lambro said. He had finished his stitching and was checking for signs of stray bleeding. "Stranger still, Colonel Maxwell. The boy learned how to read."

"What's that? How?"

Lambro moved around the table and picked up a looking glass. He placed it below the boy's nose. The mirror grew misty. The patient was breathing. It was shallow and difficult, but at least he was breathing. He lived. Lambro sighed. He put the glass back on the table. Then he straightened his back, rolled his shoulders. He sat on a chair by the table.

Victor awoke, Dr. Lambro continued as he stretched out

his feet to the fire. He awoke to a pain that sent him half mad. Indeed, it was more than he could possibly manage. Were it not for the laudanum and Victor's own knowledge of natural painkillers, such as cherries, which he shared with the kind Dr. Quigley, he would probably have died from the agony. He slept, on and off, for a week. . . .

When he finally came to—for more than those few painful seconds it took for Rebecca to feed him more laudanum—he found himself in a strange bed, in a strange room, and he was alone. His leg was completely bandaged and reinforced with some odd kind of ghostly white plaster, hard as the shell of a nut. It had been raised off the bed by a pulley and rope, so that it was almost impossible for Victor to move. A candle burned feebly on a table nearby. Beyond the great bed stood a tall wooden bureau, with three drawers, and a chest of some kind, with a lock, and a shelf on the wall stuffed with toys. And beyond that a window, barely open, and sea-blue chintz drapes. It was nighttime. A cool breeze wafted in from outside, carrying with it the smells of the street, the sounds of invisible carriages clip-clopping along, the odd voice. Something else, too. He could hear it. It was coming from somewhere below. It sounded like sawing.

Victor felt a cold fist clamp his throat. That sound! There was something about it that filled him with dread. He tried to get up, but a pain of such venom so repulsed him that he uttered an audible groan. He felt a cold sweat wash his face and passed out.

When he came to again, the sawing continued. Victor tried to cry out but his throat was so dry that the sound barely carried. He pulled himself up. His crutch stood beside him, propped up by the bed. He grasped it and swung himself around. Once again, the pain was intense, but he managed to stop himself from fainting. Slowly but surely, Victor worried the rope around his cast until the knot came undone. He pulled his leg over, gritting his teeth. The pain was horrific but tolerable. After all his misadventures, pain was something Victor had learned to accept. Indeed, over time, it had become a kind of companion, almost a friend, the herald of his Spartan endurance. Pain meant that he lived. It rooted his being.

His head felt light. Perhaps he wasn't conscious at all. Perhaps he was still dreaming.

He hauled himself up on his crutch. He hobbled with care to the door. The sound of the sawing continued. With difficulty, he made his way down the stairs. When he had reached the foyer, he realized that the sound was coming from the doctor's office. He hobbled still closer. The pain grew more terrible, the fear more intense. He felt as if his heart had somehow shifted from his chest, had slithered through his torso to his leg. It pulsed inside the plaster cast. He took another step. Then another, and another. *Yes*, he thought. The sound was coming from within. Victor slipped a hand between the double doors and heaved.

Dr. Quigley was standing by his desk. It was covered with a black felt cloth. A human leg stretched out across the surface. And in his hand, the doctor hauled a metal hacksaw back and forth across the bone. That's when the earth gave out beneath him, and Victor tumbled into unconsciousness.

* * *

When Victor awoke, he was lying on the crimson settee. He tried to move, but the pain was overwhelming. He fell back to the bench.

"Don't try and get up," Quigley said. "You shouldn't be out here at all. What were you thinking?"

Victor shook his head, trying to clear his eyes. The doctor was sitting on a chair by his desk. The leg still reclined there, still naked, exposed, strangely absent of blood. "What were you doing," asked Victor, "with that . . . that thing?"

"I was freshening the thigh. It's like a ham, you know. Sometimes you have to trim the end, if it's been out too long."

"Are you doctor or ghoul?"

Quigley laughed. "A little of both, some would say. Did I wake you?"

"The sound of a saw cutting bone, especially the bone of a man, is peculiar, Doctor Quigley."

"Is that so? I would have thought that a bone is a bone. Do you really think that it's different from wood? Perhaps so," he mused, seriously weighing the question. Then he said, "I was trying to examine the tendons and cartilage."

"For what reason?"

"Why, for you, Victor. I want to make sure you heal properly."

"I don't understand."

"Why did you bandage your owl in that way?"

"I told you. To support the bird's wing as it healed."

"Exactly. And how did you know about the bird's muscles?"

"I felt them."

"But haven't you ever examined a bird or a mammal under the skin? After it's dead?"

Reluctantly, Victor admitted he had. "But that's different," he said.

"Why is that?"

"Birds don't have souls."

"Oh, I see," said the doctor. "Forgive me, but I've never seen one—a soul, that is—during any of my many dissections."

"Are you mocking me, sir?"

"Not at all," said the doctor. He stood and walked over to Victor. "I believe you're a boy of remarkable intellect, though unformed, misdirected by circumstance, and needlessly squandered through squalor and poverty." He touched the boy's head. Then he paused and smiled sadly. He turned and stepped toward the fire, looking down at the coals. His brilliant white hair seemed to shimmer like ice in the gaslight. "You may not know this, Victor, but we are living in a wondrous age. New discoveries are being made every day, in hundreds of industries. New advances in medicine. The study of anatomy is in its formative stages. But those who are curious, men of science, are slowly unraveling the mysteries of the human physique. Diseases are revealing their secrets. Why, a friend of mine thinks that he's found the root cause of the cholera. Most people think it's the vapors, the gases that seep up from our sewers. He's convinced that it's carried by microbes, beasts so tiny they can only be observed through a microscope. Great secrets are within our grasp, Victor." He turned and looked at the boy. "But we must pry them out."

He waved at the leg on his desk. "Like gemstones, out of the earth. We must use the eyes which the Almighty gave us. The mind. Do you understand?"

"I think so."

"There is no shame in the human body. If the betterment of mankind is our goal, where's the obscenity, the ghoulishness in trying to comprehend that most delicate and wondrous of God's gifts? Our corporeal selves. These frail envelopes of the soul. Our flesh and our muscles and bones. I submit to you, there is none." He caught himself and smiled, softening. "Heal your birds, Victor, as you've learned to do. And let me do my job. Let me heal you."

·CHAPTER· 13

VICTOR HEALED QUICKLY. Dr. Quigley was amazed at the boy's recuperative powers. In but a few weeks, he was healthy enough to have visitors, a brace of most anxious retainers: Rebecca and Nico. Dr. Quigley's housekeeper, Mrs. Worthington—an irrepressibly round, handsome woman of forty with bluish-gray hair—ushered them in. Victor was ecstatic to see his two friends. Rebecca had stayed with him for the first couple of nights after the operation, but he hadn't seen her since then. She'd gone back to cadging. She'd returned to the house in St. Giles. And Nico was a thing of the streets, generally preferring to sleep outdoors, even in winter, in relative solitude, in some barrel or crate, in some alley, rather than pressed in a square knot of cadgers and beasts.

The children caught him up on the news of the rookery. Rebecca's friend, Mary, still hadn't come home. Pike had been pinched, then escaped, after stealing a handkerchief from a lady directly in front of St. Paul's. The Master had picked some new girl as companion, a flaxen-haired German. And the Happy Family of rats and cats had been the top attraction for the past several weeks, outearning even the monkeys.

After a half hour or so, Nico got up the courage to ask Victor a favor. He wanted to see if the bed in which he lay was as soft as it seemed. Victor told him to jump in and try for himself. The young boy tugged off his boots and slipped under the covers. He wiggled his feet next to Victor's. "Why, it's like heaven," he said, with a laugh. "A bed fit for angels." Then he leaped to the floor, without warning, and scurried away.

"What's the matter?" asked Victor.

"I might grow used to the softness," said Nico, with genuine fear in his eyes.

Mrs. Worthington returned with a tailor. He was carrying a bundle of secondhand vestments from the clothes shops of Middlesex. There were bottle-green spencers, and jackets of umber and ash, or of blue, and waistcoats of every description. The trousers were generally checked, or in pepper and salt. There were neckcloths and great frilly shirts.

Rebecca and Nico looked on as the tailor dressed Victor in dozens of outfits. When he was done, Mrs. Worthington had settled on three woolen coats; three cutaways—the most neutral of colors; four suits—a brown, two black, and a check; a half dozen waistcoats of various colors—three almost identical, in military gray and sea blue; two dozen white shirts, barely ruffled; a handful of neckcloths, mostly black; four sets of pants; six pairs of socks; and new work boots from E. Moses and Son of the Tottenham Court Road.

Victor stood by a looking glass and admired his form. Then

he spied Nico and Rebecca behind him. Nico was looking at him like a stranger, like a flat. Victor turned, saying, "So, what do you think?"

Rebecca reached out and caressed him. She ran a hand down his shoulder and sleeve. "You're no Shallow Lay, that's for certain," she said. "I don't recognize you, Master Victor."

"He's a gentleman now," Nico said. "He's a beggar no longer. Except for that leg."

Victor stared at himself in the mirror. He felt suddenly glum. "I'm no different," he said. "Don't let these fine liveries fool you." He tore off his top hat and cutaway. The tailor had let out the leg of his trousers to make room for the cast, and he struggled with the bulky material.

"Keep them on," Mrs. Worthington said. "You're to join Doctor Quigley for dinner. Daughter Bess and the husband are coming."

"I don't want to wear these things. Where's my real slop?"

"They've been burned."

"Don't be a fool," said Rebecca. "Count your blessings."

"But I've done nothing to deserve this, except to be crippled in an interesting way."

"Why, you ungrateful cur," said Mrs. Worthington. "Get out of here, you two." She ushered Nico and Rebecca to the door. "Out you go. Back to the streets, where ye belong. I have to dress this haddock for dinner." She glared at the tailor. "You too. All of you. Get out!" She pushed them before her. She herded them out through the door. Then she slammed it behind them and said, "Do you know where you're sleeping, boy? This room. Do you know whose it is?"

"No, I don't."

"Exactly, you vile little vagabond. How dare you take this for granted. It's his son's. The good doctor's. Or it was. Till he died."

"Died? How did he die?"

"He and the Missus," she said. "Two years ago May. An accident; so they say. Their carriage slipped off the Kent Road. It rolled over and dropped through the ice, at a bend in the river. They both drowned, trapped as they were in the carriage. The whole carriage broke through. And it slipped underwater, plucked away by the current, dragging down the two horses. Into the blackness. Under the ice. They drowned, too. They all drowned, save the coachman. He managed to haul himself free." She stopped and looked over at Victor. "Now, do you see? If you do anything, anything at all to hurt Doctor Quigley . . . Do you hear me? He's been through quite enough. I won't stand for it. Do you ken what I'm saying?"

"I do, Mrs. Worthington."

"You'd better. I look at you and I see nothing but trouble. Nothing but housework and heartache and worry. And there's been too much of that in this manor already."

"I'm sorry," said Victor. "I didn't know. About your mistress, I mean. And the boy."

"She was never my mistress. I always worked for the doctor. But the boy . . ." She could not finish. She turned away. "He would have been seven next month," she concluded. "On the twelfth." Then she moved toward the door, opened it, and stepped through. "Put on your new clothes, Master Victor.

I don't care if you hate them. I don't care if they feel like they're burning your skin. You will wear them and act like you love them. And you'll thank your new master for buying them. You may have fooled Doctor Quigley. You may have somehow wormed your way into his household and heart, but I know what you are, deep inside: a filthy, lying street beggar, a blackamoor who'll rob us at the first opportunity; perhaps kill us while we sleep; who'll wait patiently, like some spider, like a snake, until we turn our backs for an instant, for a second, and then, *wham*," she concluded, clapping her hands. "You'll slip the dirk in, just like that, when we aren't even looking. Mark my words." She stared at him from the open doorway. "Now put your clothes on and make believe you're a gentleman. We'll be eating in just a few minutes."

The door slammed. Victor looked down at the clothes on the bed. He pulled up his trousers and slipped on his cutaway. He rebuttoned the buttons in front. Then he settled his neck-cloth and collar.

He did look like a gentleman. Even his crutch, Victor thought, seemed strangely imbued with new elegance by the secondhand clothes. Worn and polished from use, it looked like an overgrown walking stick, like the staff of a wizard beside him. Victor picked up a top hat. He pressed it tight to his head. He slipped on a pair of pale lavender gloves. Then he stared at himself in the mirror again. *No*, he thought wistfully. More like a fool than a gentleman. With his cast like some overcooked sausage, blanched to tastelessness, bursting out of his trousers, bulging under his cutaway. An obvious imposter. An indelicate fraud.

Time for dinner, he thought, though he realized with sadness that Nico had walked out with his appetite.

Dr. Quigley's daughter, Bess, had been ill the day of the accident, in bed with a fever, again. A migraine had saved her. This mysterious blessing had brought her nothing but sadness, however, for in addition to her physical ailments, she now had a pustule of guilt with which to contend. She was alive, while her mother had perished. She had been lying in bed with a hot water bottle as her brother's diminutive lungs had filled up with ice crystals.

To compound her misery, she had married a drunk: a Mr. Gerald Simms-Tewksbury, who was the heir to a publishing fortune of middling proportions. He spent most of his days out to lunch with his various secretaries. A notorious philanderer, Mr. Simms-Tewksbury was constantly being lampooned in every London newspaper of consequence, save for the one put out by his family.

They sat on either side of Dr. Quigley: Bess to his right, and Gerald his left. Victor sat farther down, to the right of Bess, near the sauces. She wore a cheerful pink dress, with the great puffy sleeves of the day, drawn tight at the wrists. Her waist was unnaturally small, pressed in by a pitiless corset. And her dresses cascaded beneath her. Mr. Simms-Tewksbury wore a frock coat in gray. His waistcoat was puce, his frilled shirt snow white. The neckcloth, though lilac, didn't quite match the waistcoat.

They had already dispensed with the pleasantries. Dr. Quigley had quickly introduced his new patient as Victor of

Modena, as if he were some foreign dignitary, and Bess and Gerald had nodded and murmured their how-do-you-dos. They had been briefed about Victor at length by the housekeeper. They knew what to expect. And yet Victor surprised them. He was remarkably articulate, despite being a foreigner. He was far more polite and attentive than others his age, regardless of class or upbringing. Simms-Tewksbury kept asking him questions.

"Do you mean, boy, that all of the children bed down in the same room, in that attic, right next to each other?" he inquired.

"What choice do we have?" Victor said.

"And what do they wear?"

Bess looked appalled. "Why would you care, Gerald, honestly? They obviously can't afford bedclothes."

"I'm curious, that's all. All those children. Pressed in together with beasts, the most exotic of animals. Barely dressed. The mind boggles."

"Yes, well," Quigley said. "Boggle it differently, with something less irksome to Victor, if you please."

"I beg your pardon?" said Gerald, leaning slightly away as the serving girl proffered the entrée. They'd already enjoyed a hot soup of stewed oysters, followed by a plateful of whitebait with lemon, Victor's favorite. The entrée was turkey in jelly. A ham roast was to follow, then the pudding, a savory, and dessert.

It was always like this, Victor realized. Every dinner, at least. The Quigleys consumed far more in one sitting than Victor used to eat in a week.

"Did I tell you that Victor can already count up to one hundred," said the doctor, "and write his whole alphabet, too?"

"You did, sir," said Gerald, with graceless delight. He was fond of making note of the physician's misstatements. He pounced upon each opportunity like a cat.

"They're much like the animals, like the monkeys they train," added Bess. "Each has his own trick, to be sure."

"To read is far more than a trick. To master concepts, symbols," said Quigley. "Why, that's no mean feat. I'm proud of the boy. It's remarkable."

Victor looked at Dr. Quigley and remembered a song that he scribbled to practice his penmanship.

Attend to my ditty, attend, ev'ry one!
For I owe my existence to MOSES and SON.
I am viewed as the very perfection of dress,
And wherever I go I am met with success.
My fashion and elegance none will dispute,
But all have pronounced me a "beautiful suit" . . .

"A beautiful suit," Victor murmured. The ditty was everywhere: in newspapers; on the covers of serialized novels; on billboards and handouts and omnibuses.

"What's that?" Gerald said.

"I wanted to thank Doctor Quigley for my beautiful suit." The serving girl paused by his chair with a platter of turkey in jelly. "Thank you, Emma," he said, staring down at the aspic.

"Did you hear that, father?" said Bess.

"Warms the cockles," said Quigley.

"I'm grateful . . ."

"As you should be," said Gerald.

"More than you know, sir," said Victor. "For I know where they come from, these vestments."

"What does that mean?"

"The real cost of these shirts."

"The real cost?" Quigley asked. He smiled down at the boy. "I'm not following you, lad. What do you mean?"

"Nothing," he answered, angry now for letting himself be baited.

"And what is their cost?" Gerald asked.

"Far more than the four and a half pence they cost Doctor Quigley at E. Moses and Son."

"Why, you impudent . . ." Bess couldn't finish. Her face grew increasingly red.

Quigley held up his hand. "I want to hear what he says," he continued.

"I meant no offense, sir," said Victor.

"None taken," said Quigley. "Go on."

"They cost only pennies because thousands of women were 'sweated' to make them. Young girls like Rebecca. Hardly paid for working long hours, in frightful conditions."

"According to Nico," said Quigley, "there are one hundred and fifty thousand sewing outworkers in London. I'm sure sweating's the source of much of their anguish."

"Nico! That simpleton? That half-wit?" said Bess with a laugh. "Mrs. Worthington's mentioned him on several occasions. But Father, you don't actually believe what he tells you, do you? By all accounts, he's a fool!"

"Nico's a collector of facts, dear, though his mind may seem simple to some. He has a rare instinct for numbers."

"You see," Bess said, turning toward Gerald for help. "They've addled his brain. To say Moses sweats. The idea! Why, E. Moses and Son has done more for the shopgirls of London than practically anyone. Now Nichol of Regent Street; that's something quite different. He sweats, I'm convinced of it. His prices seem unnaturally low. At least, so I read in the *Chronicle*. Of course, I've never been there myself."

They argued for another half hour about the benefits of hand tailoring versus ready-to-wear. They argued about the new railway lines being laid down around the city—one hundred miles or so by the end of the year. Gerald had actually seen a locomotive on an elevated track, he reported as he gobbled a large mouthful of ham. Dr. Quigley was in favor of them, but Simms-Tewksbury complained about the smoke which they added to the already smog-shrouded air. They debated the talents of Miss Jenny Lind, "the Swedish Nightingale," whom Bess had heard sing at Covent Garden last Sunday. And then they argued about the propriety of seeing a singer on Sundays at all. Gerald was a Sabbatarian, a voluble proponent of banning entertainments on the Holy Day, although few working folk could avail themselves of such levities any other time during the week. For most, the Sabbath was their only day off.

After a while, Victor seemed to actually vanish. They argued on, only referring to Victor infrequently, in the third person, as if he weren't even there. Not even a person. A cipher. A symbol of working-class London. An oddity. Like one of those pineapples he'd seen at the market some weeks ago. A bit of a freak with that leg of his.

Following the savory and dessert, Victor said he was sleepy and got up from the table. The doctor and Bess and her husband were going out to the theater, but he was too tired to venture abroad. It was bedtime. He thanked Dr. Quigley for dinner and hobbled along, down the hall, out the back to the necessary. When he'd finished his business, he covered it up with some earth from a hopper. Night soil men would come by in the evening to empty the box, and to sell what they found there for fertilizer.

Victor made his way back to the house. Although he was healing quite nicely, his leg always started to throb with a dull aching pain at this hour. It was better to hide in the linens of sleep. He climbed up the stairs. He started to take off his clothes. They felt crisp and brand new, and so clean in his hands, though he knew they were used. He folded them tenderly, fingering the luxurious material. Then he looked up and caught himself in the glass. He stared at his hands. He looked back at his eyes. He flung his new trousers and shirt to the floor. *What did it matter?* he thought. Who cared where they came from?

He slipped on his nightshirt and crawled into bed. The sheets and the blankets felt rapturously soft. He pressed the white cloth to his face. He breathed in the bright smell of the cotton, freshly laundered, with that slight scent of lilac Mrs. Worthington added. *What did it matter?* he thought once again. Didn't he deserve a warm bed after all the cold nights he had spent on the cold backs of waves out at sea, in some ditch, in an alley, in some preoccupied coffin? So what if his belly were full, for a change. What harm could it do to reside—for a few nights, at least, for a few winter evenings—an arm's length from the lip of the precipice?

Victor fell asleep, strangely warm and secure. He dreamed he was home in Modena. His mother was cooking a stew and she stood by the hearth. She was stirring a cast-iron pot on the fire. She was stirring and he noticed the blood coursing out of that hole in her stomach, like a fountain, pouring into the stockpot, though she hardly seemed troubled. She was hardly aware of it as she stirred and looked up with a smile. *"Pronto a tavola,"* she said with the tiniest grin. He walked over and picked up a spoon. Then he dipped it into the great cooking pot. *Bang, bang.* He brought the spoon up to his lips. *Bang, bang!* Someone was preventing him from eating his supper. *Bang, bang,* and he woke with a start in his bed. He looked around the room. Someone was banging outside, on the window. Victor got out of bed. He could see a man's face through the glass. No, it wasn't a man. It was Nico. He was standing on the lip of the roof.

Victor went over and unfastened the latch. "What are you doing?" he said. Nico jumped through the opening. Rebecca was standing behind him. "What's going on?"

Without warning, another dark figure swept through. It was Pike. He jumped over the sill. He was smiling as he punched Victor once in the stomach. Victor buckled and dropped to his knees. Then Spendlove, Pike's cohort, appeared on the ledge. He grabbed Victor by the sleeve of his nightshirt and struck him two times in the face. He leaped through the window as Victor fell over. Victor's crutch twisted out of his grasp. Pike punched him again. Victor tried scurrying to freedom. He tried ducking and weaving, but each time he turned to escape, they struck him again. They kept punching his face. Nico tried to step in, to protect him, but they beat him away with the crutch.

They took Victor and dragged him along on the floor by his hair past the bed. They forced him to lie on his stomach as they kicked him, as they beat him again and again with the top of his crutch. Nico couldn't see any longer. Not clearly, at least. Victor's body was blocked by the bed. But Nico could still see the shadows. They danced on the wall. And both he and Rebecca could hear Victor moaning as first Pike and then Spendlove took turns, as they beat him again and again, hardly pausing for breath, as they kicked him and punched him and stomped on his face.

When he was practically unconscious, Pike kneeled down beside him and lifted the boy's bloody head in his hands. "It was me, Pike, what did this to you, Master Victor, as I promised I would. It was me and me mate. In case you see fit to remember." Then he spat in his face, on what was left of his nose. "Now it's time for a tour of this mansion of yours. See what treasures she's keepin' from Spendlove and me. More than a snuffbox or two, I would wager," said Pike. "No, don't bother to stand," he concluded. "Stay right where you are, Master Victor. If you please, sir, we'll see ourselves out."

·CHAPTER·
14

MRS. WORTHINGTON threw her hands up in disgust and stormed out of the room, slamming the door in her wake. Dr. Quigley paced in the hallway expectantly. "Well?" he said.

"Same as before. The boy won't say a thing. I warned you, Doctor Quigley. I told you he'd be nothing but trouble. I warned you."

"Yes, very well, then, Mrs. Worthington. I was warned. Happy now?"

"When you lie down with dogs, sir . . ."

"Oh, stop blithering, woman. What did he say?"

"Nothing."

"Nothing at all?"

"The innocent don't hide the truth, sir. They don't have to."

"How pithy, Mrs. Worthington. And how Christian, too. Why, I ask you, would a boy burgle a house that's been treating him kindly, and then have himself thrashed to a pulp by so-called accomplices?"

"To cover the scent, sir. He let the thieves in, most assuredly. And they knew exactly when you left for the theater."

"So did half the neighborhood. You have the habit, Mrs. Worthington, of heralding our social schedule to anyone with half a mind to listen. If you hadn't been out with your friends till all hours, perhaps the thieves would never have entered the premises."

"I'm not sure how to respond to that."

"Would you care for suggestions?"

"Oh, fiddlesticks. He knows a lot more than he's saying. How do you not wake up when somebody's beating you? It's not credible."

"Indeed," Quigley said. Then he paused. He stared down the corridor.

"He won't tell you," Mrs. Worthington said.

"We shall see," said the doctor as he moved to the door of the bedroom and entered.

Victor was lying in bed with his leg once again in a sling. At least, judging from the bedclothes, it was Victor. It was hard to tell. Between the bandages and bruised, swollen flesh, one could barely make out anything distinct or recognizable. His face was more of a suggestion than the thing itself.

Quigley had dressed his wounds the previous evening, as soon as they had returned home from the theater and found the boy, unconscious and alone. The house had been ransacked. All of the silver had been taken; most of the pewter, as well. A few pillow cases and loose pieces of jewelry. A silver thimble. An old set of gold teeth which Mrs. Quigley had worn. They had even taken some haunches of meat from the pantry, all of the liquor, and some bottles of medicine from the office downstairs, but—luckily—no works of art. Victor had been lying on the floor of his room. He had been barely alive. Whoever it was had thrashed him with such savage abandon that even his leg cast was fractured in two separate places. Dr. Quigley cleaned up his wounds and rewrapped the bandages. He replastered the leg cast as well.

"How do you feel?" Quigley asked as he moved to the bed.

Victor didn't respond. It was difficult for him to speak clearly. His head was wrapped up in bandages, and he'd bitten off a piece of his tongue in the first seconds of the assault. He nodded, instead.

Dr. Quigley sat on the bed. "Who did this to you, Victor? And why? Why would anyone act like such an animal?"

"Animals," sputtered Victor, "do not murder for sport. Or attempt to."

"Do you think they meant to kill you?"

"I don't think they cared if I lived or died. In truth, I can barely remember, Doctor Quigley. I'm sorry."

"But you must remember something."

"I don't. It's all a blur to me now. I remember seeing a face by my window. I stood up. And then . . . nothing. Then I simply woke up as you found me."

"And your dysfunctional memory wouldn't have anything to do with a certain young lady, would it? Some innocent bystander, whom you don't wish to incriminate?"

"I don't know what you mean, sir."

"Mmmm," said the doctor. "They tried to kill you, Victor. Does that mean nothing to you?"

"It means being circumspect, tight-lipped, as it were, would probably be the best course of action at this time. The old man in Portsmouth once told me that a battle is won before it begins. I need to heal and prepare myself first."

The doctor laughed. He patted Victor gently on the leg and the boy winced from the pain. "Oh, sorry about that," Quigley added.

"What will you do with me now?" Victor said.

"Do? What do you mean?"

"Mrs. Worthington urges you to be rid of me, does she not? It's hardly a secret."

"Is that what you think I should do?" said the doctor.

"I dare say, sir," said Victor. "If I could presume to be you, I'd no doubt be recalculating the cost of my medical curiosity."

"Is that all I've been doing? Satisfying my medical curiosity?"

"Has it not, sir?"

"Perhaps at one point, Victor—I'll be honest with you—you were little more than a challenge. A medical bet with myself, if you will. But since then, after getting to know you . . . I don't know, Victor. You've heard of my child, I suspect."

"Yes, I have, sir."

"Then you know that he died."

"And your wife, as I hear it, I'm sorry to say."

"Straight to the heart of the matter, as always. That's why I like you, Victor. You have but one face. It's the one you present to the world. Let me answer by being equally frank. By not being forthcoming with me now, Victor, you have shaken my trust in you. I'm sorry to say it, but there it is, plainly put. By all accounts, I should have you arrested. My friend, Nicholas Taylor, the magistrate, doesn't suffer thieves lightly."

"Yes, sir," Victor said, trying to get out of bed.

"Where do you think you're going?"

"Why, away, sir. Out of your house, before you bring on the Peelers or Dicity."

"Just a minute," said Quigley, changing his tone. "I said by all rights, or accounts, or something or other. What I meant was, that would be the usual run of events for you, Victor, wouldn't it? And you are an unusual boy. What kind of doctor would I be if I tossed you out into the street, in your feeble condition? Do you think I take my oath lightly, sir?"

"No, I do not."

"You are no longer at sea, Victor, afloat at the whim of the waves. Your fate rests within you," he said, tapping his head with a skeletal finger. "In your brain, sir. You will earn your way back to my trust. You will work for me, Victor, right here, in this house."

"But Mrs. Worthington . . ."

"Confound it, boy, whose house is this, anyway?"

Victor smiled. He pulled at the bandages which covered his eyes. "Well, based upon the best available evidence, Doctor Quigley, scientifically gathered, I'd have to confess . . . Mrs. Worthington's."

Quigley floundered about for something to say. He grew angry, then chilled, and then laughed a great laugh. "By Jove, you've got spirit. Right you are, boy." He could hardly contain himself. "You'll make a formidable scientist."

Dr. Quigley was true to his word. Far from casting him out, he drew Victor closer, to the pulse of his daily existence. Wherever the doctor went, so hobbled Victor. He served as both nurse and administrator, as chemist and personal assistant, as messenger and manservant. Victor mastered his letters with Quigley's assistance, as the surgeon prepared to see patients, poring through charts, as if they were captain and mate trying to forge a new passage together.

Doctors of the period generally recommended exercise and diet, rest and baths, together with a roster of less effective treatments such as purges, enemas, and bleeding. Arsenic-based medicines ruled the day, prescribed for a battery of illnesses, from fevers to epilepsy to rickets. Some physicians favored castor oil, others the renowned little "blue pill" that contained a staggering five grains of mercury. Lack of appetite was treated with quinine, as well as with pepsin, which was scraped from the bellies of animals.

Most Londoners preferred to self-medicate, and a cornucopia of patent-medicines was available. More than thirty thousand bottles of "Infant Preservative" were sold every year, as generations of mothers silenced their children, sometimes permanently, with this tincture of opium and liquor. Practically anything could be had over-the-counter, from morphine to opium to arsenic.

It was frustrating for physicians, who'd spent years in training, to see so few avail themselves of their skills. But physicians were expensive, and only the privileged could afford them. One could hardly blame citizens for avoiding the "bats," as doctors were called.

The majority of Londoners simply had to make do, rubbing fat on their chests for the chills, fashioning homemade poultices for boils, and drinking licorice powder for general constipation. The absence of adequate roughage, especially in winter, made most Londoners constipated. Yet the unsanitary conditions forced many to run to their privies with diarrhea. It was often a balance of naught or too much. And the doctors had little to give them. Laudanum was the most common painkiller and, coincidentally, helped bind up loose bowels. But nutrition was beyond their control, or their ken, or their interest.

If one suffered a limb fracture, as Victor had done, with a skin break or obstruction of the artery, if there were the slightest risk of gangrene, amputation was the normal routine. Yet Victor had somehow recovered. With the help of his roots and his herbs, under Quigley's fine care, he had beaten the odds.

In this age without true anesthetics, doctors could only perform a limited range of procedures. They could set broken bones and lance boils, manage external conditions, for the most part, and even operate swiftly in places they could reach with their instruments. But the lack of hygiene in the operating theater, followed by infection in recovery, meant that any kind of surgery was a high-risk proposition, even if the patient didn't perish from shock.

Despite the limitations of practice, more than five thousand university-educated men entered the medical profession between 1800 and 1830. But, according to Quigley, the men most in charge of the medical field were mediocre at best, resistant to change, and too often driven more by petty rivalry and feud than a genuine interest in science. They were called "bats" for a reason. They thrived in the dark, in the gloom of an aristocratic system of patronage. And no institution was reviled quite so tartly by Quigley than the Royal College of Surgeons. Run by a small self-selecting council of surgeons and anatomists, the College had the exclusive right to grant licenses. Anyone who wanted to become a surgeon—and, thereby, join the College—had to meet its requirements.

Though Quigley came from a wealthy shipping family, he had been smitten by medicine after a bout with a fever as a boy, and his father had gladly paid to keep the youngster at bay, at arm's length, anywhere but under his feet. In truth, he was a deep disappointment to the old man, at least until his younger brother, Timothy, had taken on the family affairs. Then he'd been all but forgotten.

Thomas Quigley wouldn't have had it any other way. He enjoyed his banishment, looking upon his fall from familial grace as a last-minute reprieve. He'd gone to school, though students rarely got their money's worth. Most teachers of medicine, if they bothered to show up for their lectures at all, were too indolent or ignorant to field Tom Quigley's questions. Besides, as the young surgeon soon learned, much of what they taught was outmoded.

So he had gone to the Brookes's school in Blenheim. Joshua Brookes was a distinguished anatomist, who had founded his school in 1787, and managed it skillfully for decades, only closing its doors due to illness in 1826. To this day, Dr. Quigley remembered the smell of the corridors. The school stank of rank meat because Brookes had a unique process of preserving his subjects by injecting them with potassium nitrate, which was generally reserved for extending the shelf life of sausages.

Once Quigley's father had approved his advancement to the Royal College of Surgeons, the next step was to become a paying apprentice, or "dresser," to a surgeon. Due to the family's prestige, young Quigley had been assigned to one of the greatest, a man of true science and skill, Dr. Jonathan Twizzlesmythe. These apprenticeships earned surgeons around fifty guineas a year—per dresser—and most had between four and six. So an annual income of more than two hundred was common. Only students who could afford such exorbitant fees could ever hope to ascend to the topmost rungs of the medical ladder. Fortunately for Quigley, despite his personal misgivings, his family's fortune ensured his success as a surgeon. Yet he still found great pleasure in tweaking the system by sponsoring young bats of humble beginnings and helping them rise through the ranks.

They lived in a wondrous age, Dr. Quigley had said, and indeed, it was true. New advances in medicine were occurring each day. Yet, despite these developments, one in three of the poor died in infancy. And while the average life expectancy in London was around thirty-five, when you factored in infantile deaths, twenty-seven was the average age people died, twenty-two among those in the working class. Twenty-two! By that measure, Victor was already middle-aged. Half the burials in the city were for children under ten. The black-plumed horse and hearse were all too familiar to the poor of the streets.

Victor studied and learned. He studied and learned and he healed, growing stronger and stronger each day. Over time, the doctor came to trust him again, sending him out on small errands with funds to buy medicines, sending him out to fetch books or machinery. They would work side by side from sunup to sunset. They would eat as they labored. They would nap at their books. Dr. Quigley treated Victor like the son he had lost. He began to reinvest all the love and the tenderness which for almost a year had eluded his heart, had vanished one February morning, swept away by that river, underneath a thin coating of ice.

Time passed, weeks and then months, and after one particularly arduous day, Dr. Quigley turned and said to Victor, "Let's break early. I'm tired. And a young man can't hold himself up in conversation during dinner if he hasn't first seen the Colosseum, or the Egyptian Hall, or Faguerre's Diorama."

The doctor called for a carriage—he leased two, month to month—and they drove for a meal at his club, and then on to Banvard's. It was beyond Victor's wildest imaginings.

The club had been so opulent and daunting that Victor had hardly touched his repast—overdone roast beef, with two burned potatoes. And he noticed the way that the waiter had stared at his dark Latin features. He had not enjoyed the experience.

But the Egyptian Hall, fronted by Sphinxes, just off of Piccadilly, had been rapturous. Spellbinding. The stuff of his dreams. John Banvard's panorama featured thirty-six scenes taking the spectator on a 3,000-mile ride from Yellowstone to New Orleans, along the Missouri and the great Mississippi. The canvas unrolled for two hours, revealing the bluffs and the prairies, the vast herds of bison, the swamps and the alligators, the slaves cutting cane, picking cotton, the Red Indian wigwams and wagon trains.

On another occasion they had visited the Royal Colosseum, built five years earlier, with its classical portico and gardens of ruins, reproductions of the Temple of Vesta and Parthenon. Inside whirred the great cycloramas, including "Paris by Night," as seen from a balloon hovering over the Tuileries. On one side, as if you were floating the Tagus, you could witness the great Lisbon earthquake of '75, with spectacular lighting effects; on the other, the eruption of Etna. Sound was provided by an enormous brass organ called the Grand Apollonicon, which thundered out Mozart. *What a wondrous world,* Victor thought. *What a spectacle!*

In the main hall ran the Great Panorama, 46,000 square feet of wound canvas depicting twenty miles around London as seen from the dome of St. Paul's. But it wasn't quite real, Victor realized. There was something missing, although it took him a moment to see it. In the end, the view was too perfect, too clear. The smoke and the smog, which wound round the neck of the city in life every day, had been strangely removed in this painted rendition.

It was the world's imperfections, Victor mused, the darkness that gave the light meaning. It was the distance from ignorance and illiteracy to the world of the word that made it so great. It was only because of the pain of his childhood that he could appreciate what he had been given. A second chance. An opportunity to create something of beauty out of all that was evil and dark. As he stood on the dome of St. Paul's, he looked out at the city of London. It may have been painted on canvas, but to Victor it had never seemed more authentic. This was the dream of the city, her promise. No matter what men saw with their eyes, this is what glowed in their minds.

Between his work and recovery, and the odd outing to some chophouse or the theater, Victor didn't have much time anymore for the cadgers. He bore no anger toward Rebecca or Nico for his beating by Spendlove and Pike, and yet they no longer seemed to fit in his world—this new world. The clothes, at which Nico had stared, had just been the beginning. Other differences soon sprang up between them, like weeds in a walkway. Over time, he saw Nico less often. They had little to say to each other. They had less in common each week.

Rebecca grew distant as well, although Victor continued to see her quite frequently, at least every few days. It was as if she were somehow embarrassed to be seen in his presence. She said that she felt like an anchor, a weight to his fortune. She would only impede him, slow down his ascent from St. Giles, and all that the rookery stood for. She said she was simply unworthy. He told her she was just being silly, but Rebecca grew sullen, removed, preferring to speak of small things of no consequence. In his heart, though, Victor feared she was right.

So he abandoned himself to his studies. Soon, Victor was reading the medical journals which Dr. Quigley brought home from the hospital each week. Soon, he was unraveling symptoms, delivering diagnoses on his own. He debated the merits of certain medical techniques and recommended new treatments for patients, especially herbal remedies based on his knowledge of plants, such as the bark of the "fever tree," *Cinchona officianalis*, and white willow. Quigley could not have been more proud.

It came as no surprise, then, when the doctor confronted Victor one night during dinner. "What are you doing this evening?" he inquired, as if Victor's schedule were some sort of mystery.

"I thought I would read," came the usual reply. He was finishing up his dessert.

"I have other plans, if you're interested."

Victor glanced up with excitement. He had grown used to the doctor's pale introduction to things. Quigley was always downplaying good news. It was part of his humor. "Perhaps," he replied. "That depends."

The doctor smiled. "I think you're ready," he said. "You've seen me do my own little experiments, and you've fainted but once."

"I told you, Doctor Quigley, I was just feeling tired that day. Not once did I . . ."

"A dissection," said Quigley. "A whole thing."

"A thing," mumbled Victor. He pushed his stewed apples away.

"A complete corpse, I believe. And a male. An acquaintance of mine is prosector. Doctor Thaddeus Crumm. His is the only progressive mind on the council of the College of Surgeons. I've mentioned him to you before. He's the one who believes microorganisms in untreated water cause the cholera."

Victor grew excited. After all of the books, after all of the hundreds of drawings, illustrations, and sketches, he would finally see for himself what lay there, right there, just under the skin. A real dissection, with other physicians and surgeons. A chance to observe like a member of the College. Victor could hardly contain himself. "Tonight, sir?" he stammered.

"Right now," answered Quigley, as he stood. "Unless you'd rather have seconds."

Victor was up and ready and hobbling along toward the door before the doctor had rounded the table. The carriage took them toward the West End, and the streets seemed particularly busy with foot traffic this night. Perhaps it was the weather. It had finally stopped raining, after two weeks of on-and-off showers. It was creeping toward spring. The pavements were jam-packed with couples enjoying a stroll before bed.

Quigley kept up a running soliloquy. He was clearly excited as well. Crumm's dissections were famous in medical circles. The man was a legendary surgeon, and a fellow Mason. His family was greatly respected and wealthy. They owned several factories in the north, making everything from everyday china to the most delicate porcelain tea services.

It was only as they turned down the street that Victor grew nervous. He was familiar with this section of Mayfair. He'd been here before. The carriage drew closer and closer and finally stopped, and so did his heart. There it was. The mansion stared out at him with its great glowing windows, like two eyes, and that tongue of a walkway, with that same Irish wolfhound on guard.

The coachman opened the door and Dr. Quigley stepped down. "This is it, Master Victor. Aren't you coming?"

The boy lingered within.

"What's the matter?" asked Quigley. "What's wrong?"

Victor crept toward the door. He looked up at the windows. He listened. Then he said, "Nothing, sir," and lowered himself to the pavement. There was no music tonight.

A pair of men in top hats and cutaways swept in from the side. They greeted the doctor and started to chat by the gate. Victor leaned on his crutch. He watched as the carriage retreated to make room for more guests.

After a moment, the doctor looked up and spied Victor. "Come along, we don't want to be late. You still want to attend, do you not?"

Quigley and his fellow physicians stared down and appraised him. Their eyes seemed to cut through his top hat and cutaway, through his waistcoat and cast, through layer upon layer of tissue and bone to the heart of his fear. "Of course," Victor said, hobbling closer. "I wouldn't miss it for anything."

·CHAPTER· 15

THE DISSECTION TOOK PLACE in the dining room. There were two dozen physicians in attendance, and they ringed the great hall in two rows, mostly standing. Their attire was formal, as if this were as much a social occasion as a scientific event. Were it not for the sprigs of spice and fresh mint which they'd stuffed up their noses to sweeten the smell, they might have been idling at some local chophouse or club.

Quigley and Victor found two places in back and settled in with a nod to the surgeon. The thing on the table at the center was male, although hardly a man. He was clearly quite young, judging from the size of his limbs, but his face was obscured by a towel.

Crumm stood by the table, dressed in an apron such as a butcher might wear, with a frock coat and checked trousers beneath. Though inordinately pale, the surgeon was handsome and thin, with a long nose and delicate mouth. His forehead was high and imposing. His eyes were dark brown, almost black, and his hair rather spare. He had a cleft at the end of his chin. All in all, in the gaslight which streamed from the great chandelier overhead, he looked rather spectral, ethereal.

Crumm ignored the interruption and continued with his lecture. "As I mentioned earlier," he said, "the subject's teeth were removed prior to his arrival and the mouth suffered serious trauma." His voice was deep and imposing, touched with an icy indifference. It revealed his impeccable parentage, his schooling at Eton and Oxford, and his languorous glide down the slide of his class. If Dr. Quigley were a four-figure man, Crumm was a five . . . perhaps more. Some said he'd soon be a knight of the realm.

"It's important," he added, "to place a block immediately under the chest." He pointed at the pillow of sand underneath the cadaver. "Just so. This causes the chest to protrude, and the arms and the neck to fall back, providing maximum access to the bounties within. Only once this is done can the internal examination begin."

Crumm stared at a young man who languished nearby. He was pudgy and pale, with a mop of blond hair. When he noticed Crumm staring, he approached with a platter of cleavers and scalpels and knives. Crumm reached out and picked one. It glimmered as he bore it aloft. "For the internal examination," he said, "a large and deep Y-shaped incision is made from shoulder to shoulder." He leaned over the body and cut through the skin of the chest. "Conjoining right here, at the breastbone," he added as he started the base line. "Extending all the way down to the pubic bone, with a slight deviation to the side of the naval." He stood up and examined his work. "If the body is that of a woman," he continued, "the incisions are made to go around the breasts so that the arms of the Y have a slightly mounded appearance. As in all things, women take the circuitous route." He grinned. "And you've undoubtedly noticed that the bleeding from cuts—if present at all—is quite minimal. With the heart still, there's no blood pressure, save what little is driven by gravity." He looked down at his apron, waving his hands like a conjurer. "You see. One can dissect and get cleaned up for dinner in minutes."

Nervous laughter erupted. Victor peered through the crowd. It was true. Not a droplet of blood had been spilled on the apron. The body had been scrubbed by a diener. It looked chalky and brittle, though the skin folded over like pastry.

Crumm stepped back and the blond man approached with a saw. He inserted the blade in the topmost incision. Then he started to saw back and forth, back and forth, with such volume that Crumm had to wait for his assistant to finish before speaking again.

"We sever the bones on the lateral sides of the chest cavity to allow the sternum and ribs to be lifted. This is done so the heart and the lungs can be seen while *in situ*, and the pericardial sac isn't damaged." The assistant placed the saw on the table and lifted the chest plate. All of the organs within were exposed, each with its own unique color and shape, each with its own special function. Victor adjusted his view. He no longer felt queasy or faint as he had upon entering the dining hall. He found it all fascinating.

The assistant stepped back from the table, holding the chest plate, and the surgeon leaned over the body again. "A scalpel is used to remove any soft tissue that is still attached to the posterior side of the chest plate," he said. "As you can see, at this stage, nearly all of the organs are visible." He waved a thin hand through the air.

"Based on the shape and development of the subject, I would guess that he was but a young man, not much more than fifteen. Maybe less. The colon is shrunken and empty, revealing he suffered from gray liquid diarrhea at the time of his death. There are signs of high fever. He was greatly malnourished. But more telling," he said, leaning forward, "is what's left of his lips. It's unfortunate the teeth were removed with an awl. The mouth has been ripped, but the symptoms are clear." He pulled off the towel with a flourish, exposing the face. The lips flopped into view. They were puckered and blue. "Cholera, gentlemen. All the signs. Violent vomiting, resulting in the tearing of the intestinal membrane. Sunken eyes. Dehydration and bloated blue lips. And yet," he continued, with an air of high drama. "And yet, there is still something else. Something which only dissection reveals."

He picked up the scalpel again. "We make a series of cuts, along the vertebral column, so that the organs can be detached and pulled out in one piece for inspection." He sliced at the cavity carefully. Then he started to pull out the organs, dropping them one by one into dishes held up by the pudgy assistant. "Each of the organs is a treasure trove of insight concerning this young man's corporeal existence. But, regarding this particular ailment, the stomach is key. Through histological examination of the intestinal mucosa, one can clearly make out tiny ovoidal bodies attached to the nerves. These encapsulated nerve endings are the result of one thing, and one thing alone: cholera. Once attacked by some sort of toxin excreted by these tiny invaders, the disease results in high fever and a great loss of fluid and electrolytes through ensuing diarrhea. The cholera's caused by a germ, gentlemen, a microbe. It's a contagious disease, and not due to some fiendish miasma. It's spread by the filth in our water. And by the end of this year, I shall prove it."

He stepped back and took a small bow as applause filled the room. Then he smiled graciously, and with a wave of the hand said, "I've set up a microscope at the end of the table, for those of you who would like to examine my samples. Look for little black nodules attached to the cells."

The gathering began to disband. A few gentlemen went up to Crumm to commend him, while others hung back for a look through the microscope. Victor pressed forward. He was dying to see. He stared at the thing on the table. The chest flaps were open, the cavity oddly vacant of organs. Despite the mint in his nose, the unique smell of death overwhelmed him and Victor hobbled along, trying to push through the crowd, trying to get to the shiny brass microscope. He was almost upon it when he stopped. What was that? He took a step closer. The object which had caught his attention was blocked by a man in a tattersall cutaway. He stepped around the corpulent figure. Right there, stuffed under the table. Victor weaved and pushed through. Then he saw it quite clearly and froze, and the room suddenly pressed down upon him. The sound of the voices grew faint. It was his hat, the one which his father had given him, and which he—in turn—had passed on to Nico. That silly little tricolor hat. He felt a cold panic crawl down his spine. He looked at the table, at the thing with its flesh flaps of skin, the torn purplish lips, the brown hair. Nico! Then it suddenly fit. How hadn't he seen it before? Despite the cadaverous skin, the sunken eyes, and blue lips, the shape and the height were identical. And that hair, that soft curly brown hair! A sudden revulsion swept through him. He felt light-headed and hot, and then cold as blood flushed from his brain. He was going to faint.

"Are you ill, boy?" said Crumm. He caught him just as Victor started to fall. "You look pale as a sheet."

The surgeon was standing by Quigley.

"I . . ." Victor couldn't spit out the words. His mouth had gone suddenly dry. "I . . . I need a . . ."

Doctor Crumm laughed. "It's outside, down the corridor, to the left. That's why they call it the necessary."

"Thank you," was all Victor could manage. He stumbled along on his crutch through the crowd. He slipped through the door.

Nico! Dead! Of the cholera! He had only just seen him last week and the boy had seemed fine. How had he come to be here, to be carved up in this manner like a roast and examined, to be hacked into pieces? It was too terrible even to contemplate. Victor looked down the corridor and remembered that evening, months earlier, when he had accompanied Rebecca to this house. He found himself moving along, away from the necessary—and the room with the carousel—toward the entrance. He needed some air. He needed to breathe! He reached for the doorknob and stopped, held in place by a tall stand of walking sticks. There were more than a dozen of them. And then the door to the dining room opened. The lecture was over and the physicians started to leave. They crowded about him.

Victor stood by the door in the foyer. He waited and watched, unable to tear himself away from the stick stand. One by one, the canes were collected. The crowd gradually thinned as the physicians departed. Then Doctors Quigley and Crumm stepped into the corridor. They were talking with a young man of twenty with dark soulful eyes and a beard who was just down from Cambridge. He was a great beetle collector, a craze at the time, and off on some voyage of discovery in the morning. But Victor found the conversation distracting. He simply nodded and waited and watched. He was observing the stick stand. A few minutes later the last guests departed. He watched as the canes disappeared one by one. The young man with the dark eyes and beard finally left, removing the penultimate cane. Quigley turned and said adieu to his friend. Then he looked down at Victor and smiled. "Was it not simply spellbinding? Do you not feel enlightened?"

Doctor Crumm turned demurely away. He appeared to be genuinely blushing. "You praise me unduly, Doctor Quigley," he said.

Victor studied the surgeon anew. He took in the tall spectral body, and tried to imagine what he looked like from behind, deleting the forehead and sensitive mouth, the black eyes and the cleft of his chin. But, try as he might, he just couldn't. Then it no longer mattered. Victor glanced at the stick stand as he opened the door. "It was a pleasure to meet you," he said.

Only one cane remained, and Victor was certain: the one with the carved ivory elephant head.

·Chapter·
16

LONDON

Victor's dream billowed up through the darkness, as if from the depths of the sea. He witnessed the body splayed out on Crumm's table. He heard the grim sawing of ribs by a pair of disembodied white hands. He watched as the rib cage was slowly removed, plucked out of the pulp, raised high like some livid communion wafer, displayed and finally set down. And then the rag was removed from the face, revealing the flapping blue lips, the sagging eye sockets, the hair. But as Victor reviewed the remains, the head turned to the side, as if strangely alive, the eyes opened, stared blankly, and he finally acknowledged the face. Mary!

Victor awoke. For a full minute he found himself unable to move, as if a paralysis had gripped him while sleeping. *What did it mean?* Victor wondered. Mary had yet to return to the rookery. She was still missing, and Rebecca was terribly worried about her best friend. And then it occurred to him. Perhaps she too had been izzied. Perhaps she had shared Nico's fate, or was about to. Victor willed his limbs to wakefulness. He sat up on his bed, took three breaths, and, with a shiver, slipped out of the covers. Despite his fear, and as much as he tried to suppress it, he knew exactly what he had to do if only to appease Rebecca's anxiety. He had no choice.

Victor hovered in the bushes in the gardens of Crumm's mansion, remembering the time that Nico had shared his bed with him in Dr. Quigley's house, and how the boy had scurried from the sheets in fear that he might grow accustomed to their softness. It was like fleeing from the sun, on those rare occasions when it skulked across the English sky. *If only Nico had spent a few more nights in comfort,* Victor thought. Life was fleeting, and moments of tranquility, of happiness and peace, were few and far between. Clear days in Nico's life had been infrequent. For the children of the rookery, it generally rained. But to have met the end he did, a thing, carved up in that display, diseased . . .

Victor pressed his back to the wall. He looked up at the evening sky, at the falling rain, at the distant sliver of the pale new moon. Even for cadgers on the fly, such a fate was peculiarly grotesque. And he had watched it all, the peeling of the skin, the sharp detachment of the breast plate, the breaking of the ribs and bones. He had stood there in his cutaway and neckcloth, like every one of those observers . . . not on the table, splayed out and gutted, but from the other side. How strange, he thought, that the source of his affliction—his shattered leg—had saved him from the streets. Without it, he would have been a cadger still. Were it not for all that pain he'd suffered, it might have been him upon that table.

The Irish wolfhound ambled up to him and sniffed his fingertips. Victor scratched at the fur by his ears. "Good boy," he whispered. "Be still." The dog gave up a yawn, and then staggered away toward the trees.

It had taken Victor almost two hours to sneak out of Quigley's house and make his way back to Mayfair on foot. Now that he was there, he wondered if he had the strength to accomplish what he had come to do. But his nightmare still revolved within him. It lingered on his skin like the smell of death on Biggs and Tipple. He held his breath. He took a step forward, then two, and stared through the rain-spattered French doors. The room with the carousel was eerily still. It was dark. No gaslight, not a lantern was lit. Victor pressed his hands around his face and peered through the glass. There was no one about.

He picked up a stone and shattered a windowpane. The dog looked over for a moment, then turned away. He seemed indifferent to the noise. Victor plucked out the pieces of glass from the frame, reached in, and unlocked the French doors. He opened them carefully. No one stirred. Nothing moved within the darkness.

He made his way past the merry-go-round toward the wall at the back of the room. The animals stared at him—the rabbits and piglets and jewel-covered unicorns. Even in the half glow of the moon, Victor could see gemstones sparkling. The animals lunged without moving, their tongues lolling out of their mouths. They waited for someone to waken them, strangely still, out of time. Victor ignored them and stepped up to the wall. He tried to remember. What had Dr. Crumm done? He had paused by this panel and pushed. But where? Victor lifted his hand. He pawed at the wall. Then he noticed a thin stream of light beaming out of a crack in the paneling. He felt with his hands. There! In the swirl of a rosebud. His fingertips stopped at a small indentation. He pushed and the panel gave way, sliding backward and off to the side. He pushed the door open.

A stairway descended out of sight. It was dark and forbidding, lit up by a solitary lantern which hung on a large wooden peg by the door. Victor lifted the lantern. A wind flicked up the stairwell, teeth-chatteringly cold, carrying with it the most piteous moan. It was human, thought Victor. The skin crawled on his neck. There, once again. A discernable howl. Then that stench in its wake, of something dead and decaying, of something yearning for peace in the earth.

Victor took a step forward. The stairs wound around, in a circle, descending for a good twenty feet, perhaps more. They opened up onto a narrow corridor. Victor looked to his left. The hall led to a room of sorts, he was certain, although Victor couldn't actually see it. He was about to investigate when he heard that strange moaning again. It was coming from there, to his right, down the corridor. He made his way forward. He held the torch high, trying to spot the grim source of that wailing. The corridor was made out of great blocks of granite, stacked on top of each other. The wailing grew louder. He hobbled along, his crutch in one hand and the torch in the other.

When the moaning stopped, so did Victor. He hovered alone in the corridor. A cold gust of wind licked his face. He drew back, he shivered. The silence was worse than the wailing. Victor could feel his heart pound in his chest. He took a step forward. Then another. And another. The corridor turned to the right. A door became visible. It was open. Light streamed from within. He wrestled with the urge to turn back, to hobble away, down the corridor, as fast as his good leg could carry him. Back to safety and his comfortable bed. But he didn't. It was clear, from his nightmare, that no refuge could be found from such evil—not even in sleep, in the warmth of his bed. He kept moving along, one step at a time, until he rounded the doorframe, until he looked around the corner and stopped.

The door opened up on a long narrow room; a hallway, more accurately, that ran the length of two cells, framed by rusty steel bars, in which Victor could see several children. They were walking in circles, or standing about, or lying down on the floor. Each cell had its own door, its own trough of black water and privy. And each was secured by a redoubtable padlock.

The occupants of the first cell—perhaps half a dozen in all—were gathered together on a blanket of straw, not far from the privy. Most were naked from the waist down, and covered in filth. Their arms and their legs were entangled together. They fought for a place by the water trough, trying to scoop up some liquid with their skeletal fingers, trying to pour it past bloated blue lips.

In contrast, the occupants of the second cell seemed strikingly able-bodied, almost fit. They too hovered together, on the far side of their cell from the dying. But they stood in small groups, or reclined on the floor.

Victor stepped into view. One of the occupants of the second cell saw him and leaped to her feet. She was wearing bright calico rags and a tatty blue bonnet. It was Mary. He saw her as clearly as she had appeared in his nightmare. She came up to the bars. She wrapped her white fingers about them and said, "Master Victor? Is it you? Or have I lost my mind, like the others?"

"It's me," Victor answered. He studied the room. No warder or turnkey. The cells were unguarded.

"How do I look?" she inquired. "Do I look sick to you? I keep asking, but there's no one around that I trust anymore. Not after what I've seen."

The girl seemed malnourished; her stomach was bloated. But there were no pustules or cankers or sores on her face. And her lips weren't discolored or swollen. "You look fine, Mary, I'm happy to tell you," he said. "Right as rain. But the others," he stammered, staring at the first cell. "The others are dying, I fear."

"It's the cholera," she said. "First one, then another. They all gradually fell. Three have perished already, that I saw. It was horrible, Victor. They shrunk into nothing. They withered away right in front of me."

Victor tried not to think about Nico. "Who brought you here, Mary? Who did this to you?" he inquired.

"I was picked up and driven away."

"But by whom?"

"By two men."

"Two men? Who? Tell me, what did they look like?"

"One was tall with bad teeth, the other terribly fat."

"Tipple and Biggs," Victor said.

"Yes, that's them. That's what they called themselves, any-way: Misters Tipple and Biggs."

"Where's the key to these cages?" asked Victor.

"There is none. Not here, anyway. The man with the cane keeps it always upon him. And he doesn't . . ."

"Shhh!" Victor said. "What was that?"

He heard voices. They were coming from just down the corridor.

Victor looked desperately about. There was nowhere to hide. Nowhere to go. Then he spied a small door at the end of the hallway. He ran past the cells. He yanked at the knob. The voices grew louder. It was Tipple and Biggs. He recognized their sonorous chatter.

"Right you are, Mister Tipple," said Biggs. "But two guin-eas is better than none."

Victor ducked through the doorway. He still carried the lantern and it revealed a small storage room with long wooden shelves, and some tools and some . . . Victor tripped, reaching out, but there was nothing in front of him. The lantern fell to the floor. He had stumbled on top of a box.

"What was that? Did you 'ear that?" asked Tipple. Then he added, "We could've 'ad eight."

For a moment, the light from the lantern kept burning. Vic-tor pushed himself back, on his elbows. He was lying on top of a casket. The light faded and faltered, then died.

"By my accounts, Mister Tipple, we've 'ad ten."

They were standing right outside of the closet, and the door was still open. Victor reached for his crutch. He used it to push at the door. It started to close.

"First eight when we brought him from Portsmouth, and now two to dispose of what little remains. Two and eight, Mister Tipple. I may not boast the brains of a Newton, but I knows how to add, sir. And that's ten."

A fear swept through Victor. They were coming inside, he was sure of it. He climbed to his feet. He tried to make out some new hiding place, but there was nowhere to secret himself. Nowhere, except . . . He looked down at the casket. Not again. He could feel the bile rise in his throat. After that last frightful journey, he had promised himself, he had sworn: never again, not until he was dead and resigned to the grave for eternity. But what choice did he have? He lifted the lid of the coffin. A wave of foul odor wafted up as it opened. Victor gagged. He could just dimly see a vague skeletal outline within, a leathery grin, the clothes rotting away on the ribs. Victor gritted his teeth. He dropped his crutch in the casket and climbed in. He could feel the bones breaking as he settled his weight on what little remained of the body. The smell overwhelmed him. He found it almost impossible not to vomit. He lifted the edge of the lid and slid it back into place, slowly but surely, slipped it over his face.

"You're just stroppy because of that mother of pearl from Belgravia. She cut you a spanking new smile, Mister Tipple, that she did."

"It's your fault," answered Tipple.

"How is that?" replied Biggs.

The door to the storage room opened, and Tipple and Biggs stepped within. Victor could see them through the crack between the lid and the casket. Tipple had a livid new scar on his cheek. It ran from his ear to his throat.

"You wasted Pike's potion on Nico," said Tipple. "It was so much more breezy when they didn't giggle and laugh about like an eel. Where's that awl gone?"

"On the shelf," answered Biggs. "Where you left it. And the doctor wasn't tickled you izzied his teeth."

"The boy had such pearly ones, it was hard to resist. He was a good-looking lad, Master Nico. Until he got sick," added Tipple. "And I say this as someone with intimate knowledge of the build of his face." Then he laughed. "Here it is. A bit sticky. Bish bash bosh it in some fisherman's daughter, if you please, Mister Biggs. Before I begin my dissection."

The two men stepped out of the closet. Then the door closed and Victor was left alone in the dark. After a moment, he lifted the lid of the casket. Nothing. Not a sound. He pulled himself up. He squirmed his way out of the coffin. Then he picked up his crutch. He felt his way back to the door. He reached for the doorknob, when it suddenly turned in his hand. It was moving!

He stepped back. The door started to open. Victor dove in behind it. He pressed himself into the corner.

"Did you open the coffin?" said Tipple.

"No, did you?"

There was a moment's pause as Victor felt the two men glance round the room. He could hear them both breathing. They were panting beside him, just beyond that thin door, and their breath reeked of finger-and-thumb.

"It would seem that he's anxious to give up his choppers, Mister Tipple, to a surgeon of your singular talents. He may be dry as a sack, but he's willin' as any brass flute I've 'ad the pleasure of diddlin' lately."

"Curb your tongue, Mister Biggs, or he'll be waitin' for you on the far side of the river. This 'ouse gives me the willies. It's always so taters in mould."

They moved around the coffin. Victor watched as Tipple stood over the corpse, as he jabbed at the jawbone, as he chiseled and heaved. *This is what they had done to poor Nico,* thought Victor. Right here, in this room. With that awl. And worse, he knew now. They had done so after knocking him out with some laudanum, handed over by Pike. The same potion they'd stolen from Quigley. They had drugged the young boy and brought him to die in this house from the cholera. Victor pressed himself into the corner. He tried to suppress it, but the thought would not leave him: Perhaps, if he hadn't been lodging with Quigley, Nico might still be alive.

Tipple heaved on the awl and the jawbone snapped out of the skull with a voluble crack. Victor started to tremble. He grew terribly cold. But he couldn't stop watching. He kept looking as Tipple lifted the jawbone and teeth and slipped them into the small leather pouch which he kept at his waist.

"Nothing to it," he said.

"Like a good bended knees, like a Stilton, they grow riper with age," added Biggs.

Then they picked up each end of the coffin and bore it aloft. They carried it out through the door. Victor could hear them as they shuffled along. They grunted and groaned. They cursed and complained. Then, all of a sudden, they were gone. They had gone back upstairs, Victor guessed. Or down that long corridor. He was finally alone.

Victor waited in silence for a few minutes more before quitting his hiding place. He peeked round the door. Except for the prisoners, no one stirred. Nothing moved in the long, narrow room. It was empty. He entered with caution, glanced about. He could still feel his heart; it seemed ready to burst from his chest.

Mary spotted him as he emerged through the doorway. She stood up. "They're gone, Master Victor," she said. "With that coffin between them. You're safe." Then she paused. She grabbed at the bars of her cell. "What do they do in that closet?"

Victor took up her hand in his own. "You don't want to know," he replied.

"Will you free us now, Victor? Will you open our cells?"

"I'll try, Mary." Victor looked round the room. There was nothing about he could use to try picking the padlock. So he ventured once more toward the closet. But, once there, he couldn't see anything suitable. Nothing, that is, but the awl which Tipple had left on the shelf. Victor eyed it with dread. It was still covered in blood and small pieces of skin. He swallowed hard. Then he picked it up with his fingertips and tried to ignore the way that it stuck to his flesh. In a moment he was back at the cell beside Mary. She watched as he inserted the tip of the instrument into the lock. But try as he might, he couldn't get the angle he needed to wiggle the tumbler within. It was useless.

"I can't, Mary. It won't turn."

She stepped back. "Free us, please, Master Victor. Or we'll die, like the others."

"I can't," Victor said once again. "And I can't break the padlocks. Even if I had something to smash them with, it would make too much noise." He started to inch toward the door.

The children climbed to their feet. Some he recognized from the house in St. Giles. Others were strangers. They gathered together. They moved toward the bars of the cell.

"Free us, please," Mary said once again. "Go on, then."

"Free us," they all cried in unison.

"I can't," Victor said. "If I try, they'll return. They'll hear us, I tell you. The man with the cane, or one of his servants. I can't." He took another step backward. "I'm sorry. I'll have to come back. Later on, don't you see? I need to get help."

"Don't leave us," said Mary. "Please, I beg you."

But Victor had already lunged through the door. He was already hobbling as fast as he could down the corridor.

· CHAPTER · 17

B Y THE TIME Victor got back to Quigley's, it was
coming on dawn. A fog poured through the streets,
hiding pockets of workmen already off to the yards, the odd
carriage or wagon, the odd oxen or sheep. Victor heard them
long before he could see them. One minute the crackle of
chatter, the boom of a laugh, or a long plaintive moo, then a
face or two bobbed into view. And all the time that he walked,
other voices resounded inside him. "Will you free us now,
Victor?" they cried. But he hadn't. He had left them behind.
Victor hobbled still faster through the alleys and streets. But
what could he do? All alone, and a cripple.

Dr. Quigley was just getting up when Victor burst through
the door. He was coming downstairs for the necessary. Victor
hobbled across to him, shouting, "I need help, sir. Please,
doctor."

Dr. Quigley stepped back. He was still wearing his nightshirt. He carried a candle aloft in one hand. "Is that you,

Master Victor? Where've you been, boy," he said, "at this hour? What's the matter?"

"They're trapped. In that mansion in Mayfair. They're trapped and they're dying," cried Victor. He didn't know where to begin. "Doctor Crumm. And that thing he dissected." Victor shook his head. Tears brimmed in his eyes. "It was Nico."

"Nico!" Dr. Quigley held the boy by the shoulder. "Your friend? Are you certain? But how?"

"Doctor Crumm."

"Doctor Crumm?" Quigley looked shocked. "Wait a minute, now, Victor. Take a moment to settle yourself." He began to lead Victor away by the elbow. "Start at the beginning," he said as they entered his office.

Quigley turned on the gaslight, they sat down, and Victor told him what had transpired that evening. He told him how he'd discovered that tricolor hat, how he'd looked down and recognized Nico, that thing. He told him how he'd gone back to Mayfair, how he'd broken into Dr. Crumm's mansion, and of the people entombed in those cells. He told him of Tipple and Biggs.

It all came pouring out in one giant torrent. Dr. Quigley let the boy finish. Then he stood up and crossed to the corner, to his cherry wood cabinet, and hoisted a crystal decanter. He poured himself a stiff drink, and a small one for Victor. "Here, take this," he said, drawing near with two tumblers.

"No. No, thank you. I must keep my wits about me."

Quigley looked at the drinks in his hands. Then he put them both down on his desk. He sighed, saying, "Doctor Crumm is my friend. Well, not exactly a friend, but close enough. He's a powerful mán. He sits on the council of the Royal College of Surgeons. And he's a Grand Master." Quigley started to pace back and forth. He couldn't sit down. "If what you say is true . . ."

"Don't you believe me?"

Quigley paused. He looked down at Victor, then turned and kept walking. "You've not always been forthright with me," he replied. "There was more to that robbery than you told me. And a lie by omission still constitutes falsehood, deception. I know that the street code prevents you from speaking, from pointing the finger, as it were. And you were protecting Rebecca, I'd wager. But the fact is, you lied to me, Victor. You dissembled. How do I know what you're telling me now is the truth?"

"But you have to believe me. I saw them. Is Crumm not in search of the cause of the cholera? Why would he set them apart in that way, all those children, in those two separate cells, save to plumb out his theory?"

"I don't know, Master Victor. I don't know what to believe." Quigley paused and looked down at the fireplace. He stared at the few faltering embers of coal. "But I know Doctor Crumm. He's a talented surgeon, and a true man of science. I find it hard to believe he'd be part of some plot to burke children. He's a gentleman, on the square."

"It would seem to me that as a member of the council, he's perfectly positioned to capitalize on the trading of things. He helps set the demand, does he not?"

"It's true that he sits on the panel that defines guidelines for qualification. The number of hours of dissection required per student. That sort of thing. He sets the bar for admission to the Royal College of Surgeons."

"There you are."

"But he's not alone!"

"I'm sure not. I'm sure there are others who profit."

"That's mad, sir. Crumm's in no need of money. His family's well-connected, and wealthy . . ."

"As you know, Doctor Quigley, simply bearing a name is not always enough to ensure the support of one's family."

"Don't be impertinent. I gave you no leave to be so familiar."

"Forgive me. I meant no offense."

Quigley sighed. "This all comes at a terrible time. I've been planning my yearly retreat to the country. And I was hoping you'd see fit to continue your studies in Kent. Even my daughter says you've become quite the gentleman."

"My friends are dying in cages and you talk of the country. In truth, sir, if you were not my benefactor, I'd wonder at Crumm's standing above you."

"How dare you?" said Quigley. He turned on the boy. His face visibly reddened as he sputtered and said, "Why you impudent . . ." But he couldn't quite finish. He looked back at the fireplace.

Victor stood up. He hobbled over to the doctor. "If this is what it means to be a gentleman, I'll have no part of it." He began to peel off his cutaway. He tossed it without looking to the ground.

"Don't do that. Please," Quigley said, bending over. He picked up the cutaway. He straightened the wrinkles with the palm of his hand.

Victor began to unbutton his waistcoat but the doctor restrained him. "Please stop," Quigley said. "You're breaking my heart, Victor." The doctor took the boy in his arms. "What do you want me to do? I can't just call the Peelers and say that the most respected surgeon in London is a murderer, a burker of children, a master of Resurrection Men."

Master's master, thought Victor, recalling what Rebecca had called him. And a molester of girls. "Why not?" he replied. "If it's true."

"Because I have no real evidence."

Victor shook himself free. "You have what I told you. My word, sir. Why would I invent such a tale? I'd go to the Bluebottles myself but they wouldn't believe me." He found it hard to continue. "It seems no one does. Perhaps I can't give you my word as a gentleman. This waistcoat and cutaway only cover so much of my skin. Will you take it as a cadger instead?"

Dr. Quigley looked down at the boy. He took his face in his hands. "As a cadger then, Victor," he said. "And a gentleman, too. I'll do what I can."

"Will you alert the police?"

"That I can't do, not without some real proof. If they ask me the root of my fears, all I have is the story you told me. And you're but a beggar to them. As you said. Just a street rat. But I'll call upon Crumm. I'll speak to him personally. I promise."

"Call upon him?" Victor wrestled away. He took a step back toward the desk.

"I'll confront him directly, and see what he says."

"When?"

"After surgery. Today. Later on. After rounds."

"You mean later this evening."

"That depends. I'm not sure when he'll see me. He has patients as well, and . . ."

Victor laughed. "It may be too late by that hour. Is this what it means to be a physician? To let children languish in pestilence?"

"That isn't fair, Victor. I'm trying to help. But there are certain proprieties, certain boundaries in civilized society. I can't simply walk into his home and accuse him."

"If you want to assist me, fulfill your desire. Now, Doctor Quigley. This instant. You can quench your curiosity, and meet your medical obligations all at once."

"What are you talking about?"

"Take off my cast."

"What's that?" Dr. Quigley pulled back.

"You heard me. Cut it off me. It's time that I walked."

"But you haven't healed yet. The breaks; they're too fresh. If I take it off now, it could mean permanent damage. You might never recover. You could lose your leg, Victor."

"That's a chance that I'm willing to take. Cut it off. I can't move in this thing. And I'll have to be limber if I'm going to go back."

"Back? Back to Crumm's house? Alone?"

Victor smiled. He hobbled across to the leather settee. "Nico was like a brother to me, Doctor Quigley. I loved him. Because he was broken, and simple, and pure. But he was kidnapped by Tipple and Biggs. Exposed to the cholera. He was burked for his body, and I watched as they opened his chest."

He sat down on the bench. He stared into space. "I watched, and I loved what I saw."

"But you didn't know, Victor."

"No, not to Crumm's house," the boy said, as he looked back at Quigley. His eyes fell into focus. "Not yet. To the house in St. Giles," he continued. "To Spendlove and Pike." Victor lifted his leg. "To Rebecca."

"She's in danger?"

"I can feel it."

"You would give up your leg for Rebecca?"

"I would give up my life, sir. Perhaps that's the difference between cadgers and gentlemen. Cadgers have so little to lose. Sometimes, all we have is our lives."

Quigley walked back to his desk. He reached into a drawer and removed a large knife, curved as a scimitar. It flashed in the gaslight. It gleamed like a small crescent moon. "I'll have to strap you down," Quigley said. "I don't imagine I can persuade you to sip on some laudanum."

Victor shook his head. "I have no time for sleep."

"This will hurt," said the doctor.

"I'm counting on it."

A few minutes later, the doctor had peeled back the cast to reveal Victor's leg underneath. It was mottled and wrinkled. It was pale and bone-thin. But it looked remarkably straight, nonetheless, and Victor felt giddy and faint. He blanched at the sight of it. He flinched as Dr. Quigley unbuckled the straps and removed the remains of the cast.

"Let me at least bind it up with some bandages. Give it a little support," asked the doctor.

"Very well."

Quigley did so. Then he handed Victor his cane.

Victor shifted his weight and swung the leg off the sofa with care. It dropped to the floor. It pulsed and it shivered with pain. He found it almost impossible not to utter a scream. He took a deep breath. He tipped forward carefully. He rocked back and forth to his feet. He leaned all his weight on his good leg and crutch, but the pain kept increasing. It stabbed through his leg, through his guts and his head like a fiery poker.

"How bad is it?" Quigley asked.

Victor took a step forward. Pain shot like sheet lightning right through him. He paused, and then stepped forward again. The pain simply couldn't get worse. It had stalled at the same level of agony. It just sat there inside him. It languished at its final intensity, and Victor was done with it. He threw it away. He was tired of suffering.

Quigley tried once again to dissuade him, but Victor was adamant. He had to find Rebecca. Immediately. If the doctor could get to Crumm's mansion, then all well and good. But if not . . . If he couldn't find something he could bring to the Peelers, then Victor would go there alone. He had to. He'd given his word to the children.

Then he was gone, out the door. He hobbled along toward St. Giles, dragging his bad leg behind him, forgetting his pain, trying to keep his mind occupied, focused. It took him almost an hour to make his way back through the fog, down the streets and the alleyways, through the maze of the rookery.

But when he finally arrived at the house, one of the cadgers informed him Rebecca had already gone out. She was begging. But where, the girl couldn't be sure.

It felt strange to be back in the rookery. Victor hadn't been at the house in St. Giles for some months, since he'd first met the doctor. The place looked far grimier, more shattered and run-down than he even remembered. So much had transpired in such a short time. He had changed, and with him, the world. His memories of Portsmouth and Modena seemed to belong to another. His life on the streets. It had all been subsumed by the world of ideas, by books and the vast panorama that Quigley had stretched out before him. This building, this street. They were no longer immobile, intransigent brick. They could be removed, and soon would be. They could be cut out of the city like cancer, like a tumor, and should be.

Victor spent the next several hours trying to locate Rebecca. He tried all of her usual hangouts and haunts, where the flats were the softest, and the people took the most abject pity on a small, pretty blind girl. He talked with dozens of cadgers. They all said the same thing: Rebecca had been there. Just a few minutes earlier. He'd just missed her. She was just up ahead. Up ahead. Up ahead. But always a few alleys distant.

It was late afternoon when he finally caught up with her. Rebecca was suddenly there, up the street, to the right. By that corner. Victor couldn't believe it. At first he thought he was seeing things, the way that she winked in the fog. One minute she was there, then she was shrouded in mist. Then she reappeared like a siren again.

He rushed up to greet her. He was calling her name when

Fortune materialized through the tendrils of fog, and that wagon, with Pike at the reins, and Tipple and Biggs in the back. So they'd found someone else to assist them, Victor thought, when he'd refused to become their bee hiver.

Victor hobbled still faster. He jostled and dodged. But the crowd seemed to gather about him, like seaweed, obstructing his path.

He cried out her name and she turned, and she looked back at him with her dark sightless eyes. She turned just as Tipple retrieved her. He picked her up—like a doll, like the child that she was—and tossed her into the back of the wagon. Biggs held her as Tipple remounted the wagon. Then he stared directly at Victor. Right into his eyes. He smiled a broad toothless grin. He lifted his top hat with a turn of the wrist. Pike flicked the long whip, struck the horse on his crup, and Fortune moved off with a lurch through the mist.

Victor hobbled after the wagon. He moved through the crowd just as fast as he could. He hobbled and hobbled, but, like the old man in Portsmouth, in the end, he just couldn't keep up.

·CHAPTER· 18

IN THE END it was all about boundaries, the lines people drew, in themselves and around them, the borders they guarded. The conventions which prevented Dr. Quigley from confronting Dr. Thaddeus Crumm were the same lines that kept all the cadgers at bay, on their side of the city: the boundaries of civilized society. They were as well-marked and clear as the streets that prescribed London's districts and neighborhoods. And then there were the boundaries within, which each person set down for himself, the lines that had apparently vanished in Tipple and Biggs. All his life, Victor had tried to be true to himself, to live by his own set of standards, that his mother, Catarina, had bequeathed him. He'd been tested and tried, dashed about by the sea, but he'd always kept his head above water. He'd refused when Tipple had offered his hand, with that half crown within it. But now, as he stood in the street, looking over Crumm's mansion, he wondered: *What lines will I have to step over tonight? And who shall I become as a consequence?*

Fog sluiced through the trees and the bushes. It lapped at the darkness, with a languorous tongue of incorporeal whiteness. It slithered its way through the night.

Victor had waited in the gardens of Crumm's mansion since twilight. Dr. Quigley had failed to produce any meeting with Crumm; the surgeon had been busy, detained. And Victor had run out of options. Rebecca had been kidnapped from right under his nose. She'd been burked, just like Mary and Nico and dozens of others. He couldn't get the image out of his head, her blind eyes retreating, sinking into her skull, her red lips turning bloated and blue.

Then the music began. Victor froze. Slowly, at first. Out of tune. He picked up the melody. The notes, they tinkled quite sprightly, yet with a haunting refrain, a bittersweet strain. Then faster, as the machine gathered speed. He pressed his back to the wall. Victor didn't want to look through those windows, at those carved wooden beasts as they circled about. He didn't want to see, but he had to. So he took a step closer, and turned, and peered through the French doors, and the spectacle unfolded before him. There was Spendlove; he was riding the carousel. He was sitting astride a gray mare. He pulled at the reins and laughed a great laugh, his mouth open and vacuous. He was cackling as he passed by the window. And beyond, at the center, rode Pike. At the heart of the wheel. He was half-buried with his head in the whirring machinery. He appeared for a moment, and then vanished as the beasts spun about. Then he came into view once again. Victor watched as he pulled his head out of the hole in the floor and said something to Spendlove, but the words were drowned out by the music. That terrible tinkling. Pike looked up, out of instinct. He stared as the French doors slid by. He noticed the figure with the crutch in the window and smiled.

Victor slipped a hand through the hole in the panel of glass. He opened the latch. He stepped through the doors.

Pike turned and shouted a warning to Spendlove. Spendlove leaped from the mare. He jumped off the carousel and dashed toward the windows.

They met in a terrible crash. Neither had slowed down at the other's approach and they thudded together like bulls. Spendlove reached out, trying to paw Victor's neck, but Victor sidestepped away. He lifted his crutch. He swung it about. It caught Spendlove on the flat of his forehead. The boy uttered a groan. He opened his mouth as the crutch fell again, shattering both his front teeth and splitting the lips in a torrent of blood. Spendlove screamed. He fell to his knees. Blood poured from his face. But before he could move, Victor hit him again on the back of the neck. Spendlove shook like a dog and was still.

Victor turned. Pike stood on the carousel. He smiled and his harelip curled back, like a snarl. Victor never slowed down. He hobbled as fast as he could to the merry-go-round. He hauled himself up.

Pike laughed as Victor tried to move closer. He matched every step Victor took. He backed farther away, through the carved wooden beasts as they moved up and down on their spindles, as the music kept tinkling relentlessly.

"Stand and fight, Master Stringall," said Victor. "Or has the pike lost his teeth? Don't tell me you're afraid of a cripple."

But Pike kept retreating. He kept backing away through the animals. Then he suddenly stopped. Victor smiled. He was standing on the far side of that hole in the flooring. Gears and drive shafts rotated beneath him, growling and churning in view. Victor hobbled around. He slipped by the flanks of an ebony stallion when Pike suddenly rushed in from the side. He ducked under his crutch. Victor felt himself thrown to the floor. He slipped through the opening. His crutch jammed in some gear. There was a terrible noise as the tip of the crutch turned to powder. Victor twisted away. He tried desperately to haul himself out of that hole, but Pike punched him and kicked at his face. Victor looked down and saw his right foot coming perilously close to some spinning machinery. He punched back at Pike without looking. He punched and he punched, simply trying to land blows. One connected and Pike slithered backward. Blood burst from his nose. He cried out. Victor pulled himself out of the opening. He hauled himself free. Pike was sliding away. He was trying to retreat through the legs of some cream-colored unicorn, studded with gems, when Victor crawled up from behind him. He picked up his crutch. He swung it around, and then down with a vengeance on top of the other boy's head. Pike crashed to the floor. He curled round the spindle at the unicorn's feet. He tried to wriggle away when Victor struck him again, and again, and again. And again, for good measure, and, just to be sure, yet again. Pike rolled over. Blood still poured from his face. Victor climbed to his feet. He stood over Pike with his crutch in his hand. He raised it above him, looking down, staring down at the pulpy red face, the lips, swollen and bloody, that eye filling up with the roots of burst capillaries. But he just couldn't do it. He couldn't, though each beat of his heart, every spasm of blood through his veins cried out that he do so. The music kept tinkling. Victor lifted his crutch even higher. He tried closing his eyes. He tried to remember that evening at Quigley's, when Spendlove and Pike had assaulted him. He tried to recall all the pain of recovery. But that music! It was driving him mad. He just couldn't do it. He couldn't. It just wasn't in him.

Victor fell to the floor. Without the distraction of battle, his leg started to crackle with spasms of pain. He rocked back and forth, trying to blot out the agony. He cradled his knee. Then, slowly but surely, Victor climbed to his feet. He felt light-headed and giddy from the spinning. The machinery kept chugging along. Victor grabbed Pike by the collar of his coat and dragged him behind him as he staggered between the carved animals. When he reached the lip of the carousel, he used his crutch to push Pike off the edge. The boy rolled, with an inexorable thud, to the floor. Victor climbed down from the carousel. He made his way back to the wall with the panel. Within moments, he had opened the portal. The stairwell revealed itself. All that darkness, and that frightful sweet smell. Victor shuddered and stepped through the opening.

The darkness seemed palpably evil, imbued with malevolent forebodings. He took a step forward. Victor fought off the horror and descended the stairwell. When he reached the next level, the feeling inexplicably lightened. He hurried along down the corridor, through the tunnel of darkness. To that light, and the door, and he was finally through.

The cells felt preternaturally still. Victor scanned them in seconds. Bodies crowded the floor in the first one. They were stacked up on top of each other like wood. But a few children stirred in the second. They were crowded together, bunched up in one corner of the cell. The few who remained. He saw Mary, in her calico rags. And her bonnet, askew on her face. And some blond girl and, finally, Rebecca! His heart leaped in his chest. Never in his life had such a small piece of ribbon, wrapped up in so inconsequential a bow, provoked such a feeling inside him.

Victor ran to the cells. He flew at the bars. He pulled at the door with his hands. "Rebecca," he cried. The children rushed to their feet. There were only five left. The rest had inexplicably vanished. Then he turned toward the first cell. The children were knotted together, still covered in filth, on the floor. They were dead, he could see that. Their blank eyes stared back at him, wordlessly crying, "Will you free us now, Victor? Will you set us all free?" They had found their release. Victor grabbed at the bars with his hands. He yanked at the door. He shook it with all of his might. But even with the help of the children, the hinges, though rusted, stayed steady. The door wouldn't budge. Nor would the great iron padlock.

"Victor?" said Rebecca. "Is that you?"

"Stand back," he replied. "I'm getting you out of here."

"It's Victor," said Mary. "He's come back to release us."

The children moved away from the bars. Victor lifted his crutch. It swung through the air. It fell with the swiftness of Mercury, and every impediment, each unfortunate turn of events, each cruel twist of fate he had weathered since leaving Modena seemed to fuse to the bars of the cell. His crutch struck the lock with an ear-shattering clang. It echoed. It rang like a bell. He struck it again, and again, and again. He struck it with such ferocity, with such force and abandon, that pieces of wood began to splinter and break off from the crutch. But he kept on beating the padlock. He pounded it over and over. He struck at it until he was spent, completely exhausted, until the crutch lay in pieces on the floor all around him, and the lock dangled down like a hanged man. Victor screamed. All of the horror within him seemed to fountain up out of his throat, seemed to spill from his mouth, like a hamper discharging its cargo.

"Rebecca," he cried as he pushed through the door. He grabbed her. He pulled her away. "I thought you were . . . I thought . . ."

"I'm safe now," she answered. "I'm with you."

The other children scrambled out of the cell. They pushed by Rebecca and Victor. They ran for the door in a frenzy, packed together like dogs. They coursed down the corridor.

With his crutch gone, Victor leaned on Rebecca. She was his leg now; he, her eyes. Together, they made up one person. Together, they struggled. They hobbled and weaved down the hall. One step at a time, they moved forward.

By the time they reached the stairwell, the other children had vanished. Only Mary had turned once to urge them to follow. Then she too had disappeared up the stairs. Victor and Rebecca could hear footsteps retreating as they followed. They inched their way forward. The music was still playing, Victor realized. Still tinkling away. That same haunting sequence, that insidious melody. Then that feeling of palpable evil returned.

Rebecca ascended the stairwell as if she could see in the dark, her blindness, for once, an advantage. They drew closer and closer to the room with the carousel. The door twinkled ahead. One more step. Then another. The music grew louder. One more step and they came to the head of the stairwell. The carousel spun into view; the horses and unicorns prancing; the rabbits and pigs on the run. And beside them, by Mary and the rest of the children, with his top hat and cane, in his shiny black coattails, stood the surgeon, Dr. Thaddeus Crumm.

"You!" he said as his eyes fell on Victor. "I know you. You're that boy who observed my dissection. Quigley's charge."

Rebecca and Victor crept forward. Pike and Spendlove still lay on the floor, still unconscious. Mary and the rest of the children cowered off to the side. They were trapped between the doctor and the doors to the garden. So were Rebecca and Victor.

"Why did you come here?" asked Crumm. "How dare you interfere with my work!"

"You call this work?" replied Victor, sweeping an arm toward the children.

"There's an epidemic smoldering in Sunderland. As we speak, the cholera is expanding its grasp. Thousands will die if we don't find the root cause and a cure."

"But they're children," said Victor.

"They're cadgers," said Crumm. "What's a few worthless beggars next to thousands of citizens? It's the natural selection of things."

"There's nothing natural about this. You're a ghoul, Doctor Crumm. You're a burker of children. And a molester of girls," he continued, glancing down at Rebecca.

"A what? Oh, I see," Crumm replied. "Now I remember. You're that driver, that cripple who took her away. Hartley's one-legged coachman. My, but haven't you come up in the world." Then he laughed. "And I thought you had some moral objection. You're in love with the girl. How winsome. How sweet!" He took a step forward and said, "But whatever's happened to your cast, Master . . . Master . . ."

". . . Victor. I had it removed."

"Prematurely, it seems. Pray tell, Master Victor: What for?"

"To make it easier to kill you," Victor said.

"Is that why you came here? To kill me? To rescue your damsel and these miserable children?"

"That's right." Victor hobbled along with Rebecca beside him. They inched their way toward the carousel.

"I thought you were a doctor in waiting. A healer of men."

"I thought you were, too. And look what you've managed to do."

Crumm smiled. His deep-set black eyes seemed to twinkle. He picked at the cleft in his chin. "There are times when some tissue must be sacrificed to ensure the survival of the patient."

Victor laughed grimly. "In that case, Doctor Crumm, I'll consider you cancer." He turned toward Rebecca and said, "Get ready."

"For what?" she replied. Victor grabbed at the lip of the carousel and swung them both up to the platform. Then the merry-go-round spun away.

Doctor Crumm cackled. He glanced down at Spendlove and Pike on the floor for a moment and then faced the carousel. "Where are you going, Master Victor?" he said. "And without your crutch!"

"I have dozens of them," Victor answered. He pointed at the shiny brass spindles around him. The bars rose and fell as the carousel turned, and with them the jeweled wooden animals. Victor hobbled along, in between them. When he reached the opening in the carousel floor, he stopped. "Take a good look, Doctor Crumm," he continued. Then he hoisted Rebecca up on the stallion beside him. She clung to the animal's neck, her face pressed to the carved wooden mane. "This is the last time you'll ever see Rebecca on this infernal machine."

"Rebecca? Is that her name?" Crumm smiled. "True enough, I'm afraid, Master Victor. But there will be others. Many others. There are always more girls in the world. There's an endless supply of the poor and the desperate, of those who'd give practically anything to get in from the cold for a night. You should know, Master Victor."

"I'm waiting."

"For what?"

"For you to decide if you'll come up and finish us, and leave the children behind to run off while you're busy, or if you'll try and herd them below, and risk losing Rebecca and me. In either event, your secret is out. You're finished, Doctor Crumm. After this, the only dissection you'll attend will be yours."

Crumm laughed. He took a step closer to the carousel. "Do you genuinely believe the police will take the word of a few worthless cadgers over Thaddeus Crumm? Let them run, I don't care. Let them cry to the heavens. Or will they stay to assist you, Master Victor? Aye, that's the question. Will they come to your aid, or run the first chance they get? Let's try an experiment, shall we? As two men of science." He moved away from the children toward the edge of the carousel. He lifted his cane. "Go ahead, then. You're free. Run away, little children. Run back to your miserable lives."

The children looked at each other. Mary glanced over at Rebecca and Victor, and then turned away. Without answering, they slunk toward the doors leading out to the garden. And then they were suddenly gone. The fog had consumed them.

"Now it's just you and me, Master Victor," said Crumm. "And your lady. I think my point's proven." He curled a thumb toward the doors. "And these were the children you were trying to rescue." He cackled again. He leaped on the carousel. His cutaway billowed behind him as he swung into place on the platform. "Strange that I should be teaching a boy of the streets such a lesson."

"If this is the price that you place upon life, sir, I'd rather be the poorest of cadgers than a king among gentlemen. Come and face me."

"Or a prince among surgeons? Don't be a fool, boy. I can help you. Quigley's not the only one with powerful connections."

"Come and face me."

"Oh, to hell with you then." Crumm threw off his top hat and charged through the animals.

They came at each other, Victor hobbling along with one hand on the spindles, and Crumm at a furious run. The surgeon lifted his cane. He swung it down like a rapier, but Victor leaped out of the way and it bounced off the flank of some unicorn harmlessly. Crumm lunged at the boy. Though bigger and stronger, he found it difficult to reach Victor through the legs of the animals. Each time that he fastened a hand upon him, the boy scurried away.

They wrestled and crawled through the beasts. They inched toward Rebecca, who sat all alone on her stallion. She was trying to follow the fight with her ears, but the music kept tinkling relentlessly. Her head bobbed to and fro as she attempted to pick up the strains of the struggle.

Then they came to that hole in the platform. Victor hovered beside it, hunched over and winded. He waited and watched as Dr. Crumm swung around. The surgeon leaned over, he grabbed at his ankle, and Victor felt his fingers upon him. They clawed at his skin. His leg pulsed with pain but he kept it in place. He wrapped his hands round two spindles. He pulled himself forward. Since his leg had been crippled, Victor's arms had grown unnaturally strong. Crumm tried everything he could to loosen the boy, to yank him away from those spindles, but Victor kept dragging him forward. Inch by inch, toward that hole. By the time the doctor could see what Victor was doing, it was too late. He watched as his coat tails slipped down through the opening, as the shiny black linen unfurled like a flag. There was a great renting sound, but the material held. Crumm lurched backward. He screamed as his legs vanished into the hole. Victor held onto his fingers, but the doctor

/ 208 /

kept disappearing. He screamed and kept screaming as the sound of the gears did their handiwork. Blood oiled and gears ground. Crumm's face twisted in agony. "Help me," he cried. "Help me, for God's sake, it's crushing me."

Victor tried with all his might to pull Crumm free, but he couldn't. The physician kept shrinking from sight, dragged down by the gears of the carousel. Crumm held out his cane. Victor grabbed at the end. He hauled back on the elephant head. The doctor held on for dear life as the gears ground beneath him. He held on as he screamed, when someone reached out and plucked at his fingers. They slipped from the cane. Victor looked up. It was Mary! She and the other children were standing around them, looking down at the hole. They waited and watched as Crumm vanished from sight, as the gears clogged and choked and ground to a halt, as the tinkling faltered and died. A great plume of steam escaped from the engine. The carousel slowed. One after the other, the animals abandoned their desperate charging. They started to coast, to slide to a standstill.

Victor climbed to his feet. He turned toward Rebecca. "It's over," he said.

Just then, the door to the hallway burst open. Men charged through the door. They wore leather "pot" hats and stiff-collared blue coats. The first of the Bluebottles looked at the carousel, at the carnage within, and pulled out his rattle. He twirled it to call for assistance. Moments later, more Peelers appeared at the door. Behind them ran Quigley. The doctor dashed up to the carousel. "Victor," he cried. "Victor, are you all right?"

Victor looked down at the hole in the platform. Nothing was left of Dr. Thaddeus Crumm. He'd been ground up like some kind of sausage. Only the odd piece of flesh, the odd bone, and a great splash of blood served to distinguish his point of departure.

"Let me help you," said Quigley as he climbed up on the platform.

"I can manage," said Victor. He leaned on a spindle, took a step. Then he suddenly hesitated. "I thought you weren't coming," he said. "That you didn't believe me."

Dr. Quigley held back. He watched as Victor took his hand off the spindle. "I received an invitation, soon after you left, announcing another dissection," said Quigley. "Of an interesting thing. A blind girl," he added. "As soon as I read it, I knew you were telling the truth. I called on my friend Nicholas Taylor, the magistrate. The Peelers caught Tipple and Biggs with a corpse not two blocks from here." Then he paused, and looked down. "Is that Crumm?" he inquired.

Victor nodded. "What's left of him. No matter what he did—to Nico and the rest of the children—he didn't deserve such an ending."

"Yes, he did," said Rebecca. She looked down at the hole. Though sightless, her eyes plumbed the depths. Then she reached out a hand. "Get me out of here, Victor," she said.

Quigley watched with fascination as Victor inched his way toward Rebecca, one step at a time, without touching the spindles, without any assistance whatsoever. "Why, Victor, you're . . . you're . . . How's the leg?"

Victor smiled. "It seems to be holding up, Doctor Quigley.

If I can learn how to read, why shouldn't I learn how to walk again?" Then he turned to Rebecca. "Let's go home," Victor said.

"Home?" she asked him. "Not back to St. Giles? Not the rookery?"

"No," Quigley said with conviction. "You shall never return to that horrible place. Neither you, Master Victor, nor Rebecca. You shall come to my home in the country. Unless, of course, you've grown tired of being my dresser."

"Did you hear that, Rebecca?" said Victor, as he helped her slide down from the stallion. "To a cottage somewhere in the country."

"With a room for two young ones upstairs."

"And a sky that goes on for eternity."

EPILOGUE

SEPTEMBER, 1852

VIRGINIA WATERS

SURREY, ENGLAND

MOONLIGHT SWEPT THROUGH THE VALLEY, revealing the vast panorama of forest and field, the hedgerow, and that pond at the base of the hill by the village. Dr. Lambro stared out of his doorway. He watched as Colonel Maxwell disappeared down the lane.

It had grown late. The boy on the table slept peacefully. Somehow or another, he had lived through the surgery. But only time would tell if he'd survive the infection that would undoubtedly follow. Lambro sighed. In the end, he thought with no small sense of irony, it was they, physicians, those referred to as bats, and not grave robbers who should be called Resurrection Men. Then he looked once again at the sky. At least, he considered, it had finally stopped raining. By dawn, the sky would be clear.

Lambro stared through the doorway at the valley below and remembered a night, long ago, when he'd gone to the Royal Colosseum in London and witnessed the same panorama that had so entranced Victor: the churches and monuments; the stone quilt of rooftops and chimneys; the vast throbbing vista of the greatest city on earth. The funnel of the great tornado of the empire, as Biggs had once called it—Biggs, who, like Tipple, had finally found peace at the end of a rope. Lambro closed his back door. In the end, he thought, looking down at the boy on his table, it wasn't the wonders of the Colosseum, the spectacular wealth and technology, the miracle of London that marked England as a great nation, a mighty civilization. Nor was it her advances in science and medicine. In the final analysis, the true measure of cultures was the way in which they treated the least among them, the poor and the weak, the insane, disenfranchised, imprisoned. It was not the top of the world, but the bottom which more truly defined it.

Dr. Lambro stared down at the boy on his table. "Nico," he said. He stood there for a moment longer. Then he lit another candle and made his way from the kitchen, down the corridor, toward the stairs.

Lambro's children were sleeping in the room at the back of the landing. He watched them from the doorway as they breathed, as they lay there together in bed, tucked up in their blankets. It was the softest bed he'd been able to find in the county.

He was about to close the door when a noise made him turn. The candle flame flickered. It almost blew out. Lambro pricked up his ears. Someone was moving about in the kitchen. Someone was walking the corridor.

The doctor stepped from the doorway. He hoisted the candle. He looked down the stairs but the stairwell was dark. He couldn't see more than a few feet in front of him. "Who's there?" he cried out. "Who is that?"

"It's me."

Lambro breathed a sigh of relief. It was his wife, coming home from the neighbors. She glided along the dark corridor. In this space, in this house in the country, notwithstanding the blackness, she moved as though she could see.

To enter the world of *Resurrection Men*, go to www.tkwelsh.com and key in the following code—NICO10 (N–I–C–O–One–Zero). Explore hidden sections of the *Resurrection Men* site. Unearth new secrets about the book. Play games and challenge yourself with puzzles and mind-benders. Help Victor rescue Rebecca. Design your own book cover, cast your own *Resurrection Men* movie, and interact with other T. K. Welsh fans. The world of the body-snatcher is only a mouse-click away.